Also by Kimberly Labor

I Dream of You Still: Early Years in Bath

Beatrice Aflame

Philippa Feast

Paris Broke Me (In)

The Voices of Saint Bede's

✠

A NOVEL BY

KIMBERLY LABOR

Amazon Kindle Direct Publishing

Amazon Kindle Direct Publishing, USA

ISBN 9781693197055

Front cover image: From William Holman Hunt – May Morning on Magdalen Tower – Wikimedia Commons

Back cover images: photographs by the author

Printed in the United States of America

"It is difficult—at least, I find it difficult—to understand people who speak the truth."

~ Mr. Beebe in *A Room with a View,*
E.M. Forster (1908), chapter one

The Voices of Saint Bede's

1 ✠ April 23

"She comes in and out of consciousness," the doctor said softly.

"I see," I answered, tears coursing freely down my cheeks, slumped in the chair beside my sister's hospital bed, my luggage at my feet.

I had arrived into New York from Los Angeles on a red-eye and taken a taxi from the airport straight to Saint Raphael's Hospital, Manhattan, in the early dawn hours. Walking into the neurointensive care unit with heart pounding, I had found my dear Frances lying asleep, pale, her long dark hair streaming on either side of her lovely face, her body attached to a bewildering array of machines, tubes, and monitors.

"We're not sure of everything yet, but the concussion was clearly severe, and she's got some nasty cuts and bruising also on her arms. A staff member at her church—you know big Saint Bede's Episcopal Church in Harlem—found her collapsed on a cement path last night as he was passing from the courtyard over to the side entrance of the church. The MRI and other tests we have run, however, do not show the extent of swelling or damage we might have expected, and there is no need for a ventilator at this point. We have her on IV fluids, of course."

I nodded, feeling dazed. "So…?"

"She's young and otherwise very healthy and I have every hope that she will fully awake and recover quite soon. The next few days will be critical. We'll of course monitor her very closely and make whatever adjustments in her care that may become necessary. Of course, you can visit whenever you want, day or night."

"Yes, thank you. Thank you so very much," I murmured, as Dr. Benedetto Lasso slowly took his leave.

*

It is evening now. I stayed at the hospital about three hours and then, feeling I was going to drop with fatigue, came to Frances's apartment, where I am now, slept for about four hours, then managed to eat something. Thank heavens I thought to bring the spare keys that Frances sent to me about six months ago when she agreed that I should be her emergency contact. I went back to the hospital in late afternoon, but nothing had changed. I've called Matt, taken a shower, and sat and cried for a good while.

I know no one here in New York besides Frances, so I've decided to start writing this journal to keep track of things and give myself a place in which to vent. I'm most certainly going to stay here until Frances is well and back on her feet and they have figured out exactly what horrible thing happened last night.

It's too late now to return to the hospital, but it occurs to me that I might glean something useful if I scroll back through Frances's and my many emails these past few months.

*

January 3

Dear Frances,

Your descriptions of the Christmas Concert and the big Eve service there at your grand old New York church were well worth the wait. Glad you've gotten back into singing this past year, and your gang there sounds very interesting, especially the tall handsome young student conductor Caspar Lang. Ah, what a treat for the sopranos and altos! I remember from my (brief!) high-school dancing days the jockeying for attention among us dewy-eyed students when a new ballet teacher came to lead class—although of course you could never be entirely sure whether he was straight or gay. Are you sure this new young buck is not gay? He sounds very dashing. You've told me the older, head music director Averill is gay. So he is Caspar's professor and boss?

You are quite a bit older than young Caspar, my dear, yet I sense a distinct thrill in your descriptions of the interactions you have with him... I was going to caution you, but then—why not? Why is it perfectly socially acceptable for older men and younger women to get together but not older women and younger men? Time will tell, then.

"Hold your horses!" I hear you erupting as you read me—ha, ha! I know you're "done" with all that, my dear—you've made that clear. You are relieved to be free, free, free, and devoted solely to The Arts, both in your

admin job at the Connexion and in this esteemed chorus. Totally with you, that is, I do understand. Still, dear sister, nothing wrong with a little attraction—just enjoy it, as I think you are doing! Glad you enjoyed performing the various anthems, the Bainton, Stanford, Britten, etc., and that the little kids' segment went well. So you have a professional choir in residence there, too. Must be a big church, your Saint Bede's! But then you are now in New York, the Big Apple! I acknowledge that it was the incomparable arts scene that drew you there, but brrr, I could not bear those northeast winters, and I wonder how long you'll want to put up with them. You're only forty-eight, but having just turned fifty-three I can tell you that older bones start to feel the cold more—you remember the two-week marketing conference in Boston I attended last March for our juice biz. I started to creak and ache and couldn't wait to get back to balmy Santa Maria!

Matt just walked in—he sends you his love—and I need to start dinner. I'll let you go. Keep me informed of it all! Through your emails I'm truly enjoying, from the comfort of my quiet, sunny home, the life of the big-city artist!

Love, Phoebe

*

January 20

Dear Phoebe,

Well, you have guessed that I have become a bit fond of our young conductor. Just have to share the latest with you!

Arrived at church Sunday afternoon after tromping across ice and snow wearing clunky thick-soled clogs and had put on my cranberry choir robe. Caspar and I crossed paths in the choir room, smiling, and he said enthusiastically, pointing down at my tremendously ugly, practical footwear, "I like *those!" I laughed and replied, "These are L.L. Bean clogs. For brutal winter. I'm nothing if not practical!" He is so silly, and so kind. This was his way, simply, of greeting me.*

"Now," he said to the gathering singers, "it is very slippery and unsafe out there, so if anyone wants or needs to go home, just do it." (He mentioned having written an email about this an hour before rehearsal time, but all of us were already en route *in the subway or on the road, and I for one had not even seen that email!) He added, "And if you leave, be sure to do it dramatically," at which point—I think he knew it would be crazy me who would react, standing in full view in front of him in the middle of the room—I turned abruptly toward the door, melodramatically thrusting an arm into the air before me, and cried, "I'm leaving!" We hooted with laughter! "We're good at that here," Caspar remarked. Drama, he meant.*

Then before we began to sing, an unexpected, very deep theological and philosophical exchange occurred. The soprano beside me, Zoe, mentioned some sordid newsbit and remarked that "beauty is only skin deep" and a mere trap to the unsuspecting. Caspar, whose leitmotif *happens to be "Worship the Lord in the beauty of holiness," has a special conviction about the correlation of beauty with every other virtue, I suppose because his profession is to produce beautiful music. He'd responded to Zoe, "You know, Beauty actually is the answer." I chimed in, and from there, it was a dialogue between him and me:*

Frances: Not Beauty alone. You need Truth, too. There is false beauty, you know.

Caspar: [Turning to me.] But real Beauty is *Truth, no?*

F: [Pause to think.] Yes, all right.

C: And what is Truth?

F: [Pause to wonder: has this turned into a Socratic dialogue? Or a catechism lesson?] Goodness. Goodness to all.

C: And what is Goodness?

F: God.

C: Ah, so it all circles around to this. God! A lot in our world could be solved with this.

F: Yes!

Talk about a light, pre-sing chat! I think in fact I let myself be led astray, however, since if Beauty and Truth and God are completely synonymous, why do we have different words for these things? I think Dostoevsky actually got it right when he said in The Brothers Karamazov, *"Beauty is mysterious as well as terrible. God and devil are fighting there, and the battlefield is the heart of man." (Check it out, Phoebe—Book 3, Chapter 3—and tell me what you think!) Still, there is something about Caspar's charm and fuzzy idealism that makes it enjoyable to be led astray—for a brief moment, that is. Caspar's interests—one of which is a series he is attending at Saint Agatha's Roman Catholic Church on Contemporary Film and Traditional Values—are touching. He seems to be a sincere young man, and we all are growing fond of him. Yet I can't help but wonder whether he's completely alert to current affairs: does he not notice that much about the present state of his church is not at all beautiful or godly?*

Warm-up fun: Caspar wanted us to shake our index finger in front of our face in order to focus our voices. He shared by the by that he'd faced this wagging finger a lot from his mom as a kid, and, turning to me, added, "Because I was bad!" I immediately concurred, "Me, too." After we did this exercise, he reflected on what kind of parents we all would be, based on our finger-wagging styles. "Very stern, some of you," and he frowned, glancing my way. I laughed, as I'd been wagging very energetically. "Some of the men," he went on, "were rather..." and he let his shoulders sag. "Pushovers!" I cried. Funny, funny, all so much fun! Caspar instigates these opportunities for general hilarity, but I am one of the few singers who actually jumps in and makes ripostes. I can tell Caspar enjoys all this a lot. Lately he's been commenting on how serious the choristers are, that they don't seem to enjoy doing his entertaining warm-ups, and he likes that we adults are more light-hearted.

In the church as we were assembling in the choir stalls, the incomparably effusive Averill Page, the music director, a short, stocky, bespectacled, balding, springy sort of man aged about fifty-five, came over to me at the end of the soprano row, smiling his winning smile. He embraced me warmly. As the chorus erupted into laughter and appreciative comments, he proceeded down the entire row of sopranos, giving hugs and kisses. I saw young second soprano Sherry a few chairs down looking wide-eyed and commented to her, "This is the warmest, fuzziest place I've ever been!" I wonder whether Caspar also receives hugs from Averill from time to time: I would imagine so, of course, but I think it is easier for gay men to give public hugs to women than to men. I glanced at Caspar's face as Averill was making his hugging procession, and it was serious, unsmiling. What was he thinking? I believe that Caspar's father is in his mid-seventies: was he perhaps an emotionally distant father during Caspar's childhood? Caspar is, I believe, about thirty-three. Might he be gay, you suggest, Phoebe. I don't think so...but then again, I'm not sure. He's got quite striking good looks, his father a second-generation Dane and his mother a native-born Mexican.

The evensong singing went very well, no mistakes, all lovely. Averill is a seasoned conductor and organist, very clear with his direction and easy to follow.

Afterwards, back in the swirling rehearsal hall as we were all disrobing, turning in scores, and bundling up again, Caspar wished us safe travels home. I told him that, never able to pass up Bach, I was staying for the guest organ recital, to which he responded, "Terrific! See you in there!"

One more memorable bit: I saw Father Radcliffe Sauer in passing, the priest in charge of arts and liturgy, a rather somber and tense-looking man with black-framed glasses, and I mentioned to him that some of us were getting over nasty colds and coughs: might the incense not be swung quite so close to us singers? He smiled a peculiar sort of smile and said, "Thank you for that suggestion, dear," and then turned away.

Once I got home, I had a little dinner and a glass of red wine—I was cold and also over-excited from the lovely afternoon. Later, I read Caspar's earlier email to the group. Here it is, and our ensuing emails.

Hi Chorus,

The weather has changed unexpectedly and we are concerned that the grounds of Saint Bede's are not currently safe because of the heavy coating of ice. Hence we would like you all to STAY HOME out of harm's way. If you are already on your way, you are naturally very welcome to join in singing for evensong. But if not, we advise you to avoid the streets and sidewalks and skip this service.

If you are already on your way but concerned about the ice, please call me on my cell and I will assist you walking down the drive.

Caspar

Dear Caspar,

It was so kind of you to offer to help people walking in the icy, slippery conditions. You are quite a gentleman, and I think you are rather rare these days!

I am glad I did not see your email until I got home here, however—glad I left for the subway at 1:20, because it is always such a joy to rehearse and sing with you and Averill and Doug, and I would have been sad to miss today! And I enjoyed that quick but very profound exchange we had on beauty and truth and God. I think it is so wonderful that you ponder these subjects deeply. I hope that life will give you all that your good heart desires.

Thank you so much for all you do for us in the chorus, Caspar. See you Thursday at rehearsal.

Frances

Hi Frances,

Thank you for the message! Today was grand, and I'm glad so many of you were there. It was well worth the extra effort despite the abysmal weather. And yes, beauty, truth and God are subjects we all need to discuss more often. I think a deeper understanding of them would solve a lot of today's anxiety!

Wonderful to be working with you in chorus. See you Thursday!

Caspar

Phoebe dear, I've gone on much too long as usual, but I wanted to give you a taste of the fun we have at chorus. Caspar is adorable, but I'm beginning to suspect that he finds me younger than I actually am—ha ha! People have thought I was about thirty for the past twenty years now, lucky me! Back when I was thirty, I thought if I ever got married I would want to have just one child, a boy, and how wonderful, I thought, if he turned out to be musical—a radiant piping choir boy! Maybe I will become a sort of "auntie" figure to Caspar—how lovely that would be!

Long enough e-letter for you? Better go. Looking forward to your news.

Frances xo

2 ✠ April 24

Spent most the afternoon at the hospital today, sitting dejectedly by Frances's bedside. Although still in the neurointensive care section, she has been moved to a small private room with a window. During the long hours I was with her, she did not awaken once, but Dr. Lasso told me that earlier that morning she had opened her eyes briefly and moaned. I feel an infuriated sort of sorrow and helplessness.

But at least she is alive, for we received another bombshell today. A police officer came to Frances's room around 3:00, Detective Pandolfo Morales, and talked with Dr. Lasso, a nurse, and me. A *dead body* was found in Saint Bede's! A maintenance man discovered it yesterday morning at the foot of the baby grand piano in the big hall where they apparently rehearse and where they also feed the homeless on Saturday mornings. My mind just reeled, and my first reaction was of extreme frustration that Frances had ever decided to move to New York, leaving sunny, peaceful southern California behind. The body was that of a woman, but the detective could not give us her name yet. So now

Frances, when she awakes, will be *doubly* involved in a police investigation! *Dear God.*

I'm sitting here in Frances's room as the sun is setting, my stomach in a knot. I'd better go down to the cafeteria and get a cup of tea. As Frances sleeps, I've been scrolling back through her many email letters, her many descriptions of happy Thursdays and Sundays with the chorus.

*

February 10

Dear Phoebe,

At last, time for a proper response after the very short but successful Portugal Connexion business trip. I certainly don't handle jetlag as well as I used to. But what a joyous welcome back to chorus Thursday evening! Big hug from Caspar, and he chose me as soprano in his SATB quartet to model the sort of voice quality he wanted in the chorus! At the end of rehearsal I gave him my little present, standing at the piano as singers were dispersing. Unwrapping the little rosary from Fátima, he marveled and said, "You've found the key to my heart, because I love the rosary!" I gasped, hopefully not too loudly, and asked, "Do you?" I remarked that I treasured my German great-grandmother's old silver and amethyst rosary. I think that despite the age difference, Caspar and I are soul mates of a sort. A blissful return to rehearsals!

Then Sunday, a full day at Saint Bede's, starting with another hug and on to rehearsal and singing in the morning service. Caspar and I exchanged funny words over opening a window for our overheated choir hall: "Yes, dear" from him, and then, playing along, "Thank you, darling" from me—we got a few raised eyebrows from some of the altos and sopranos! In the afternoon I attended evensong, conducted by Averill, followed by a beautiful a cappella *concert of sacred music by a small guest choir that Caspar introduced as assistant choirmaster. As I was heading out afterwards he stopped me and said, "I want to introduce you to someone." My first thought was, Aha, the girlfriend at last. But no, his mother! I was tickled and honored. "How very nice to meet you," I said warmly, taking her hand. "This is Frances," he said. I heard myself say to her, "You have a wonderful son. We all love him a lot in the chorus. He's a real spark." Caspar put an arm around his mother, a slender woman with long dark wavy hair, and said that she was his joy and inspiration—so touching. He then flew off to congratulate the singers, and I stayed chatting with his mom for five minutes. She is from Mexico, met Caspar's father when he was on an archeological dig near her town long ago. She is about my height, and as I looked into her deep brown eyes, which so closely resembled Caspar's, it was clear that she adored her son fiercely. She appears to be in her mid-to-late-sixties, many lines on her still very pretty face. As we stood chatting, she told me how she had taken Caspar as a very young boy to a downtown church to see whether he would be interested in singing with the choristers. He was, and musically "things really took off for him." When he turned just sixteen, he was asked to serve as an assistant conductor for the church choir, and he loved it! At that point, despite his love also for world geography, he pretty much decided he wanted to pursue a career in music. I asked Mrs. Lang whether she also was a musician. No, she just loved classical music and had wanted to expose her children to it as much as possible. She added proudly that her other child, Caspar's older sister, played the French horn professionally.*

Well, what an honor to be introduced to Caspar's mother! I wonder why exactly he did that, and what she thought of me. For the first few moments, during which I was feeling delighted, I thought I noticed a slight narrowing of Mrs. Lang's eyes, as she eyed me. I have heard that Latin mothers can be very possessive of their sons, and after even this brief conversation with her, it was clear that she cherished him deeply. Maybe she also was fooled into thinking I was younger than I am and that I was a contender for the affection of her handsome son. I think so, actually. Great mirth! It is admittedly nice to be thought in my thirties, but on the other hand, I get uncomfortable in these situations. It will all come out in the wash, as they say. I may start calling myself Auntie Fran during chorus rehearsals—now there is an idea. No more romantic entanglements for this older bird! But I confess that the little tingle of warmth I feel with this charming young man is enjoyable and I hope it lasts.

Love, F. xo

*

February 17

Dear Phoebe,

Perturbation! You know the regular joys of chorus. Well, about a month ago, I enthusiastically wrote out a $300 check to support the music program at Saint Bede's and put it in a nice greeting card, which I handed to Caspar after rehearsal that Thursday. I just checked my bank statement, and that check has still not cleared! I *know large churches can have rather disorganized and underpaid staff: maybe someone in the office put it in a cubby hole somewhere with other checks and then delayed going to the bank to deposit them all. We'll hope. I'll call that office tomorrow morning.*

Today, Sunday, our community chorus combined again with the professional choir as we sang the morning service. This choir is excellent, each singer a soloist in his/her own right. They tend not to mix with us ordinary folk, not because of snobbishness, just because we have no rehearsals in common on a weekly basis, have never been introduced, and we are not seated intermingled. We all typically sing the psalm and the major anthem of the day. The choir sings additional, more challenging pieces—often an ancient introit setting right at the beginning and, later on, another anthem. On the Sundays both groups sing, chorus gets warmed up in our rehearsal hall by Caspar and Doug, the accompanist. (Have I mentioned Doug Brinte? He's excellent, also an organist like Averill. Quite young, maybe only thirty. English, married, and with two kids!) The choir warms up and rehearses up in the church itself. Then for about thirty minutes before the service, the chorus and choir together rehearse and run all the day's pieces in the church, under Averill's expert baton. The choir has their own robing and music storage room back down below, so once the services are over, whish, *we all return to our lairs to put everything away and then head out and home.*

So all this to say that today was the first time I actually made the acquaintance of one of the pro singers. It was on the subway platform after the service, waiting for the train. One of the tenors and I recognized that we both sang at Saint Bede's, and we said hello and began to chat. His name is Vincent Flaxtin, a tall fashionably coiffured blond early music specialist. He approached me first and said that he'd discerned my voice among the chorus and found that it was very good: how very sweet of him! I thanked him. He is lined up to sing at the Met soon in an early Handel opera, rarely performed, Almira. *Pleasure to meet you, sir!*

So all is basically well, or will be once I figure out what happened to my check. I'm sniffling a bit today: have I told you that Saint Bede's uses incense on Sundays? The old high-church practice of swinging and thrusting the censor full of smoldering incense at the altar, the clergy, the congregation, and the choirs. Splutter-cough! A bit antiquated, in my book, and our chorister den-mother Caroline tells me she is concerned for some of her tender young ones, one of whom has asthma. Ah, what we endure for the sake of glorious Tradition, right? Sometimes it does lend a mystical, magical appeal to our services—if we have enjoyed an imaginative and uplifting sermon that day, of course, which is not always the case—but really, I think for health reasons, it should be discontinued. Not for me to say, but maybe Caroline will speak up about it.

How is Matt's shoulder? And why do men persist in believing they are invincible, even past the age of fifty?

All for now.
Love, Frances

*

March 1
Dear Phoebe,

Good to get all your news and know Matt as well as the orchard are doing fine once more.

Back to my favorite topic, Saint Bede's Chorus. That missing check I told you about: I called the church office, explained it all, and the next day their secretary Everild Dunne emailed me to say that no one had been able to find it in their offices. Hmm. Which led me back to Caspar: I'd handed the check directly to him that Thursday evening. Could he have lost it?? Sinking feeling. So I emailed him, explained it all as simply and calmly as possible. That was a Tuesday morning. I got no reply that day, or the next. Thursday evening, then, I set off for rehearsal as usual, and arriving early, I found Caspar and asked him about the check. He was gracious and friendly as always, and very sorry, unsure what had happened. For the first time, I felt a dip of confidence in him, and I sensed he was distressed, too. He promised me he would look through all his pockets and papers and see whether he'd somehow misplaced it. I reminded him that I'd put it inside a greeting card: did he remember opening that card? "Card," he pondered. "A card... No, Frances, I'm not sure I do remember the card. What kind of card?" I said it was of medium size with a floral pastel design and a quote about eternal friendship by Beethoven. He looked down his long lean legs and shuffled in place. "I'm not sure, actually." I felt crestfallen, Phoebe, as you can imagine. "Don't worry," he then assured me brightly, looking directly into my eyes, his handsome face and earnest expression winning me over. "I'll look for it right after rehearsal, and I'm sure I'll find it. I'm so sorry if I stashed it somewhere and forgot to take it to Everild!" The sight of his confident, friendly eyes banished all clouds from the scene and I felt assured and happy once more.

Rehearsal went well as usual: we started a lovely Stanford Magnificat *and* Nunc Dimittis *and a few other pieces, including the Vivaldi* Gloria, *which is on the docket for Easter. Caspar, in his expansive way, at one point asked, glancing at me, "If Vivaldi were a drink, what kind would he be?" "What?" I asked, surprised, and he repeated his amusing question. I thought a moment and said, "Champagne!" I was thinking of Vivaldi's bubbly yet potent style, very joyful and uplifting. Caspar repeated, "Champagne. Yes!" He smiled and added, "I like it that we are on the same wavelength on these things!" How adorable! Caspar does have a way of winning people over—but of course, talented and dashing young people learn to use their charm from a very young age, I'm sure, and with the hovering devotion of their dear mamas, they get better and better at it as the years go on! Still, I'm happy to be won over. I'll let you know as soon as Caspar finds my check.*

Better go now—soup boiling on the stove!

Frances xo

*

March 7

Dear Phoebe,

Well, crisis averted, happily, just in time. The missing check saga: I'd hoped to hear something from Caspar the day after that rehearsal, but in fact five days went by. Friday, Saturday, Sunday, Monday, Tuesday… Fortunately, only pro choir and the children sang at the Sunday services that week, our adult chorus not on duty, so I stayed home and took a long chilly walk in the park, read Iris Murdoch, and then that evening watched Masterpiece Theatre. By Wednesday, the day before our weekly rehearsal, I was feeling pretty low: I'd contributed a very generous amount of money to Saint Bede's music program, the check had been lost, and now no one seemed really interested in seriously looking for it. How was I going to handle this wretched disappointment now? To my immense relief, Thursday morning around 11:00 I got an email from Caspar saying he had found my card and check in a Mozart score he was preparing for his course! Hallelujah, Jesus! He said he'd already walked it over to Everild, and he apologized profusely for his oversight. I zapped back a short email expressing my relief and thanks. As you can well imagine, Phoebe, I felt a huge weight lifted and immediately began to look forward once again to rehearsal later on.

As I entered the rehearsal room, Caspar was already there and came straight over to me and swept me up into his arms. "Again, really sorry," he said. I was delighted and overwhelmed.

"No problem," I said, coming back down to earth and looking up into the smiling brown eyes of the spirited Mr. Lang. "All's well that ends well, as they say!"

"I would like to take you out to coffee, Frances, to make up for this," Caspar added.

"How very nice!" I replied, smiling with gratitude and amazement. "You're on!"

"How about right after rehearsal tonight?"

"Why not?"

Can you believe it, Phoebe, your forty-eight-year-old sister out with a gallant thirty-three-year-old music student and conductor! Thank God, as we say, for the great hair and skin genes we seem to have inherited from Mother: no grey, almost no lines! I admit I was feeling rather giddy as Caspar and I walked down several blocks to a quiet, lesser-known café and sat down at a corner table. It was about 9:20 when we arrived and there were only a few other customers scattered about, none in close range.

For a fraction of a moment, as we settled in over our coffees and raised our eyes to each other's, I think we each felt a twinge of panic: with the fifteen-year age difference between us, what were we doing out for a little "date"? But of course, Caspar still might not have realized my age, and I was suddenly feeling very secretive about that. I said quickly, silently to myself, You are the older, wiser person here. Be that.

"So you are preparing the Coronation Mass *for your choir at school?" I asked brightly. Yes, he was, and we focused on the glories of Mozart for a few minutes. I then asked, "Do you like working with Averill? Is he very demanding?"*

Caspar smiled, looked briefly away and then back, and said, "I'm very *lucky to be working with him. He's brilliant, amazing. Yes, demanding, but he also gives a lot of positive feedback. After conducting class we often go out for drinks and more discussion."*

My eyes widened for a split second, but then, of course, I know the world of the arts—dancers, artists, musicians, all very social, and many very fond of the after-work drink. I in fact reminisced aloud, "Back when I sang in California, sometimes after rehearsals a little group of us would go out for drinks, the conductor included, and he could really throw them back!" We laughed. "It was fun," I added. "Great memories of bygone times."

"I can throw a few back myself," said Caspar boastfully. "And Averill definitely can!" We laughed again and raised our coffee cups in a toast.

"Actually, I understand the need to relax after working hard—everybody finds their own way to decompress, it's only natural. I don't think a little alcohol is a bad thing. I like red wine myself."

"I do, too!" said Caspar. "Averill goes for gin and tonic."

"That's what my California conductor liked," I mused. "He was gay, too, coincidentally." Everyone knew Averill was gay—no secret there.

"Upstate where I did my master's, all my male classmates were gay," Caspar remarked. "I was the only straight man there." (I thought to myself, That point now cleared up!) "In fact," he went on, "there was some pressure socially: 'If you stay, gay by May,' we used to hear."

"No! Really?" We smiled. I remarked, "Maybe that was a little bit uncomfortable for you? I've worked around gay men for years and years, but of course for a straight woman that's no big deal, even rather nice, no pressure. But among men, well, what's it like? Averill seems to like you a lot."

Caspar looked briefly away again but then met my gaze frankly and said, "Averill is very professional. Yes, I think he likes me, but he's worked now for decades with so many students. He also has a partner, a percussionist here in town, you know the one who played in the

Christmas concert. There's no problem with Averill, it's fine."

"Oh, that's good," I replied. Then, deciding to sound him out on his choice of churches, I asked, "What do you think about gay priests? I know you are Roman Catholic. We've all seen the horrendous stories coming out over and over again about pedophile priests abusing boys. I think if your clergy were allowed to get married, and if women also could become priests, that whole sordid problem would be solved, don't you?"

Caspar stiffened up slightly and shifted in his seat. "It's horrible, of course, the abuse of kids," he began. "There's no excuse for priests who do that. But celibacy for priests, think about it: isn't it remarkable and beautiful that men should want to devote their entire lives to God? To God and the service of his church? Most priests are good men. It's the few who are not that get so much press."

I was silent and thoughtful, recognizing this lofty, idealistic streak in Caspar, which comes out also from time to time when he is rehearsing us in chorus. His motto, in fact, which he puts sub-signature-block on all his emails, is, as I think I've told you, "Worship the Lord in the beauty of holiness." I reminded myself that he was only thirty-three and had been raised by an adoring, over-protective, and fervent Catholic Mexican mother.

"Yes, I see that: such devotion is admirable. But you know, Caspar, I am quite a bit older than you"—oh! somehow I heard myself say this, and well, Phoebe, as you know, the truth will out, *it always will!—"and over the years I've attended many churches. I even attended mass for a couple months at a little Catholic church back in*

California, just because I adored the peace of that little whitewashed adobe chapel and the kindness of the priest. But think about this, Caspar: most priests, from very devout Catholic families, decide to go to seminary when they are very young. They are idealistic and pure-hearted. I grant you that! Their hearts are in the right place. They want to serve God, to give everything to God."

"Yes!" cried Caspar. "They do, they really do."

"Yes," I continued. "I believe that, too—for the most part. But at that age, do they really know themselves? I have to say, I really don't think so. They complete seminary. They begin pastoring a church, or working as a hospital chaplain, or whatever. They work around ordinary people, men and women and children, old and young. And then, boom! One day they fall in love. I mean, it's only natural. Ye gads, *the poor priest thinks,* this is terrible. This cannot be! *They have been inculcated with the belief that they are above and beyond the 'temptations' of the world, as they see them, thanks to their special priestly relationship with God. But you know, it just ain't so."*

Caspar could not suppress the smallest of chuckles. I grinned.

"You get the point. The so-afflicted priest then goes on to do one of several things. He tries his best to stifle his natural sexual urges. He casts himself on the floor, prone, before the altar in prayer and self-sacrifice. Very beautiful," I said, not able to keep a mild tone of sarcasm out of my tone. "Or he goes straight to his own spiritual advisor and talks it all over—and the two of them together go cast themselves prone before the altar."

At this point both Caspar and I burst out giggling.

"I am being horribly naughty," I observed, as we smiled into each other's twinkling eyes, taking sips of our coffee. "Or, Caspar," I resumed more seriously, "some priests, suppressing all they can and, as it were, muddling on, find that their affections spill out after all. They just can't help it. Some start secret affairs with those poor devout single young Catholic women who attend daily mass. Some, who are gay in orientation but vowed to celibacy, break down and begin to have relationships with other gay men, or, here's the horror, take advantage of the young boys in their charge. They just do. And it's all a damned shame. I mean, there no doubt is a very small minority of men who are genuinely celibately inclined—and personally, I really have liked various nuns and monks I've met during my life. But most *men—and women—are built for marriage. They just are. It's the way God created humans, designed to find mates and keep the species going."*

Caspar had sat back and crossed his long legs in order to fully observe me pontificating on this subject, and I could see a small flame of admiration burning in his eyes. "Well, Frances," he said, "you speak well, and I do understand. But for me, the example of priestly celibacy is still a beautiful thing, a noble symbol to the world of how great God is, how some can give all their love, their entire life to him. And as for homosexuals, you know, usually there is some upset in their childhood, and therapy can really do marvelous things."

I was secretly rather appalled to hear Caspar allude to gay conversion therapy, but I nodded. I was in part impressed with the idealism of this devout young musician, even though, fundamentally, I knew he was wrong, wrong in the big picture of how churches actually worked, and wrong about how human beings were formed and ultimately behaved.

"Caspar, your idealism is…admirable," I said, smiling sincerely at my young friend. "But I think celibacy should be a choice, not a requirement, for being a priest. I really do. I also think gays actually cannot help being the way they are, but obviously any abuse of children is horrific. And I think women should be allowed to be priests: a person does not choose their sex, after all, and women are just as smart and compassionate as men."

"Jesus' disciples were men," murmured Caspar, "and in the long tradition of the church, women were never priests. This is okay with me." My heart really fell to hear him say this, but I tried not to show it. "There is a lot, a very lot, that women can do, and do *do, in the church without being priests. And think about the fragmentation of the family these days! My dear mother stayed home to raise us, and I think that was a very godly thing to do. And think of Our Lady, the Blessed Virgin, her supreme role in the church and her example to all women of pure, selfless love."*

"Yes, I take your points, Caspar," I said, realizing we were much farther apart in religious and social matters than I had thought before our coffee outing. Knowing I enjoyed working with him musically, I didn't want to come out too strongly in criticism of his views. "Well, we all are entitled to our views. This is America, after all!" I said. We smiled.

It must have been after 10:30 at that point, so we paid up and walked back up the block, towards the subway. To change the subject completely, as we knew we ought to do, Caspar asked, "What are you reading right now? And who is your favorite author?"

"Oh, gosh, my favorite author! So many. Impossible to choose. I love the nineteenth-century novelists—Dickens, Zola, Hugo, Tolstoy, Dostoevsky, all of them. Plus many of the more modern writers like E.M. Forster, Iris Murdoch, Doris Lessing, Margaret Atwood, Alexander McCall Smith..."

"Whoops, too big a question," Caspar joked. "I forgot your degree was in literature." I laughed merrily and elbowed him lightly in the ribs as we walked.

"I'm reading E.M. Forster right now," I said, cutting to the point. "For the nth time, A Room with a View. *It's fantastic, so insightful—you would like it, too, Caspar, I know you would. Beauty and love are its big themes. What are you reading?"*

"Music history and theory," he said. "Comprehensive exams coming up. Not much time lately for novels, but one of my favorites is Quo Vadis *by Henryk Sienkiewicz—have you read it?"*

"No. I've heard of it but never read it."

"Oh, you must! It's set in the time of Jesus, in Rome. A long intricate historical tale. It's wonderful."

"Okay," I said. "I'll put it on my list. And I'll email you the titles of my very favorite books."

As we got to the subway preparing to go different directions, Caspar and I faced each other and he said, "I enjoyed that, Frances. And I'm so glad I found your check. I really apologize for misplacing it for so long! And it was very generous of you. Thank you."

I was moved and replied, "I'm glad it turned up. Very glad. All's well that ends well!"

We gave each other a big hug and then waved as we separated. "See you on Sunday!" we each cried.

Well, Phoebe, that's the story for now! I'll let you make of all that what you will!

Love, Frances

*

March 11

Dear Phoebe,

"Adorable. That's what you and Caspar are—adorable. Are you sure the fifteen years' age difference is important? Just think about it."

My dear sister, have you gone mad? Well, I suppose that must be the way some people see it, looking from the outside. Even the chorus members I think have started to titter among themselves, seeing the hugs and jokes that go on every rehearsal between us. But no. Really no. Caspar is sweet and very handsome, but you know he's not 100% on my wavelength after all. His conservative Roman Catholicism truly is not my cup of tea. He also tends to cultivate, I'm seeing, a rather flashy urban playboy image: he posts photos of himself from various galas and fundraisers he attends, surrounded by sleek seductive-looking young women in shiny dresses, and then he enjoys all the comments from his male friends who remark on how he is so often surrounded by beautiful women! NO, thank you. He is young, and maybe this is just what young, bright performing artists and conductors do, present a flashy cosmopolitan image to the world in order to attract attention and further their own careers. Classical music, you know, is now "sexy."

Actually, it's interesting, when you think about it: Caspar is genuinely very religious, devoted to his mother and to the Virgin Mary, a regular mass-goer; and yet he also presents himself publicly surrounded with a sort of harem of lovely, satin-clad young women! Didn't some famous psychologist write about all this...the Madonna and the Whore syndrome? That some men worship their mothers so much that they grow up seeing women in only two lights, either as saintly mother figures, or as alluring, sinful women of the night? Forgive me—that is no doubt carrying things too far with young Caspar!

Let me move on. I think I see a new romance developing between one of our chorus altos, Claire Jozan-Prue, and one of the professional choir basses, powerful, azure-eyed Victor Boindon. The other evening just before rehearsal started, I felt a tap on the back as I came up from the water fountain: Victor, curiously, since as I've told you, the pros don't rehearse with us on Thursday evenings. "Oh!" he said. "Sorry, I thought you were Claire!" She and I are about the same height, both with long black hair. I wrote to you about her a few months ago, Phoebe, you'll recall, when we were both commiserating over the Saint Francis Day service.

I smiled at Victor. "I think she just went into the robing room to check that her robe has not been stolen again—it went missing last week." He thanked me and strode purposefully towards the chorus's robing room. I glanced discreetly in that direction as I headed back to the rehearsal hall and saw the two of them standing nose to nose and talking in low tones. How sweet, I thought—they look good for each other!

Well, Easter is coming, and the birds and the bees are starting to do what they always do in springtime—ha! Have I told you that Saint Bede's houses some pet peacocks on the grounds? Three of them, who are allowed to strut around freely during the day once temperatures warm up. In fact, as the day's light lengthens in March, at the start of chorus rehearsals we sometimes hear them crying out in their distinctive ways, which always makes us smile. It happened this past Thursday evening, in fact. "Wha-wha!" we heard, just as Caspar and Doug had finished warming us up. I'd had a glass of wine earlier at lunch and was still feeling a bit buoyant. "Wha-wha!" I imitated, and Caspar looked over and smiled at me.

"There they go again," he said.

"Ah, spring!" I cried.

"You know what happens in spring," *Caspar continued, and the chorus laughed. Another loud peacock cry wafted in through the open window.*

"The last blast of the evening," I remarked.

Caspar interpreted this in his own way. He said thoughtfully, "That's probably what they are doing out there."

I had not actually intended that precise meaning, but I didn't want to appear shocked or make light of Caspar's observation, which in fact I found rather innocent and sweet. So I simply said, "That could well be."

He and I both looked away, realizing we'd put our dialogue on stage for the whole chorus to hear—as in fact happens rather often lately—and Doug took up the baton to begin rehearsing the Vivaldi.

Must go now—but next time I'll tell you more about Caspar's mother: I spent about thirty minutes chatting with her after the service last Sunday—poor thing was in one of those orthopedic boots, had sprained her ankle badly! Since Caspar was running around greeting people and taking care of after-service business, I sat down to keep her company. She's quite a live-wire, likes to chat, had stories to tell. She seems to like me!

Later, dear.

Love, Frances

3 ✠ April 29

A full week has gone by, and Frances has not awakened! But a couple of the older women chorus members have tiptoed in to visit briefly, tiny fragile ladies in their seventies, bless their hearts, as well as her boss from the Connexion. Yesterday I actually met the much-chronicled Caspar Lang, who came bringing sympathy, he said, also from Averill and Doug, the two other music directors at Saint Bede's. Caspar's looks are very striking, with his penetrating brown eyes made more intense by his prominent brows. He has a charmingly crooked nose, a wide pleasant mouth, and abundant shoulder-length black hair roughly parted at one side and forming a lush and shifting frame around his face. His long, lean figure was dressed smartly in white shirt, jeans, brogues, and form-fitting soft wool jacket.

After sitting at Frances's bedside for a few moments, both of us somberly slumped forward gazing on her sad, unmoving form, I suggested we go down to the cafeteria for a cup of tea. There, he told me that the woman whose body was found the day after Frances was admitted to the hospital was named Claire.

"Claire from the chorus?" I gasped, and he confirmed.

"You knew her?"

"Frances mentioned her in an email. We are very close—we write a lot. She really loves the chorus, tells me all about it, the pieces you sing…" I did not want to divulge too much and so stopped myself a bit short.

"Chorus is on hiatus right now because of what's happened, but the professional choir is continuing to sing at services, just…just to keep things going. This is all a complete and utter disaster, and so far, none of us understands a thing. The police have talked with every chorus and choir member and all the clergy and staff, but I for one have not gotten any updates yet. We're all very sick at heart. Frances…she will recover?" he asked softly.

"Dr. Lasso thinks so. But the longer this coma goes on, of course…"

"We are all praying hard for her," said Caspar.

"Thank you. Thank you sincerely." I felt moved, and we both paused to drink from our paper tea cups.

"Caspar, Frances has told me a bit about you. I understand you are a student at the Breconford Academy of Music?"

"Yes, doctoral student."

"You aim for the grandest of stages?" I regretted my choice of words after I asked this question but decided to let it go.

"No, actually. I'm not an organist or pianist, and not a vocal soloist. I'm just a lowly conductor type," he said with a rueful smile, pushing a rich mass of hair behind one ear, "and I'm realizing that without more up my sleeve, I will probably end up in a school or college teaching job, hopefully a good one."

"Oh, I'm sure you will land a very good job! Frances has told me what a spark you are, how enthusiastic and devoted to music."

Caspar smiled gratefully at me, and I saw what Frances saw in him, quite a winning and attractive young man. But I had serious concerns to pursue. "Caspar," I ventured, "do you have any idea what on earth lead to Claire's death and Frances's fall? I'm sorry, but I need to ask you this. Were there any enmities among chorus members or others at Saint Bede's?"

"Goodness, no! I don't think so," Caspar replied immediately. "We all get along great, a warm environment there."

"Frances mentioned one of the priests in an email, one specifically in charge of liturgy, and she said he was a rather bitter-looking man."

"Father Sauer? Radcliffe Sauer. He doesn't smile much, it's true! I don't know him well at all. He, Averill, and the rector meet weekly to plan the services. I think he's from Boston."

"And Averill: you've worked with Averill now for a while?"

"Yes, since I enrolled at Breconford last fall. My doctoral advisor and my boss at Saint Bede's. A brilliant organist and conductor, fine man."

"You're very fortunate," I said.

"I am," Caspar agreed, but shifted in his seat and looked away.

"I'm sorry to ask so many questions, but as you can understand, I need to find out what happened to Frances, how she fell. I don't understand how she could have fallen so hard on her own in the spot they found her, that path leading out from the side of the church. It was not raining, there were apparently just two steps there—I've looked at a plan of your church online. Unless perhaps she was running from someone..."

Caspar remained silently frowning and reflective. "Sounds like it, I agree," he finally murmured.

"That door," I continued. "That's the door most the singers exit after your rehearsals?"

"Yes, we rehearse in the basement hall—it's actually a semi-basement with many windows—and then, sometimes, for the last thirty minutes right up in the chancel. Because the big main church doors are locked except for service times, we all use that side door on the church level coming and going from rehearsals. Either Doug or I locks up downstairs at the end of each rehearsal, and I think a maintenance man checks all the church doors later. That side door closes and self-locks: it's got one of those...what are they called…hydraulic door closers at the top—easy. You come out onto a path leading to the courtyard situated to the south of the church, as you probably saw, with the rector's home, a school building, and one other small building where various staff live. It's divided into apartments. And then there is a short drive and walkway westwards, down to the avenue."

"Okay," I replied, nodding. "I can visualize all that. Are there restrooms near the chancel, too?"

"Yes, on the north side, down one flight of stairs from the chancel. Those are the ones the congregation tends to use. There are more restrooms in the basement proper, on the south side, next to the big hall. It's kind of an interconnected warren down there: the hall, various robing rooms for the singers, the acolyte room, and maybe a couple other rooms I've never been in! There are stairs at both north and south ends. As I've said, the singers—and we music staff—come in at the south church door for rehearsals, and we almost always go straight down those south stairs to get to the hall."

"Is there an exit to the exterior from the basement hall?"

"Hmm, yes, I think so, but I've never seen anyone use it. We all come and go through the church's south side door. In fact, thinking about it, the big front church doors are open only around service times, used by the congregation. We hold services seven days a week. But the choirs sing only on Sundays, unless some special event is on the schedule, of course."

"Frances has told me you hold weekly chorus rehearsals on Thursday evenings, I think from around 7:00 to 9:00?"

"Right."

"Detective Morales told us that a maintenance man discovered the body, poor Claire, on Friday morning lying at the foot of the hall's baby grand piano. But someone discovered Frances late the previous evening, Thursday, near the side door of the church, along that path. Thank God he did, otherwise she might have lain there for..."

"Yes, horrible. Yes, that's what I've heard too. I think it was Father Blum, the pastoral care priest, who discovered Frances—he lives on site and was returning to the church sometime that night—he'd left a book in the pulpit and was going to retrieve it."

"Father Blum," I mused, nodding. "I haven't met any of the priests, you know."

"Phoebe, I should have mentioned this earlier: I led only the first hour of that Thursday rehearsal, then left to attend a special fundraising event down at Saint Patrick's—I'm Roman Catholic, you see. Doug directed the rest of the rehearsal on his own. I texted with him later on, and he wrote that all had gone fine, and that because his English auntie was in town, he'd ended rehearsal about five minutes early and dashed off. Of course, he was as shocked as the rest of us when he eventually heard about Claire and Frances."

"Doug is…?" I began hesitantly.

"A genius. Above us all, actually, there at Saint Bede's. Came to us from the RAM, Royal Academy of Music, London. The ultimate gentleman. Married to a university anthropology professor. Two little kids. The kindest, gentlest, smartest, and most ethical guy you will ever meet."

I nodded. We both remained silent in thought for a moment. "Well, I know the police are working on it," I said. "And when Frances wakes up—" and here my voice faltered, since in fact I was not sure she *would* awake, and I felt my heart dropping out of me. But I bucked up: "—maybe she will remember something, or have some insight into all of this."

"Yes, I hope so," Caspar responded immediately, and as we met each other's frank gaze across the grey hospital cafeteria table, I perceived that the concern on his face was genuine.

"We should go back up now," I said, collecting and crushing our empty paper cups in my hand. As Caspar and I were hauling ourselves to our feet, Dr. Benedetto Lasso walked into the cafeteria, looked around a moment, and walked straight over to us.

"Phoebe," he said with some urgency. "Frances is awake and in some emotional distress. Will you please come up with me to her room?"

Caspar cried, "Awake!" and I exclaimed, "She is?" Looking quickly down at his phone, Caspar added, "But I've got to run, I need to start a rehearsal with the kids soon. But keep me posted!"

"Of course!" I said, my pulse now racing with the thought of Frances's recovery. "It was so nice to meet you, Caspar, and thank you for visiting Frances. I'll be in touch." Caspar squeezed my hand warmly.

Back in Frances's room, Dr. Lasso, a nurse named Violet, and I gazed down on my wide-eyed sister, tears streaming down her pale cheeks.

"Frances, my dear, my dear! Oh, don't cry. You are safe. I'm here. You are going to be fine."

Frances's eyes looked frantic. "Phoebe…" she moaned, lifting a hand toward me.

"Yes, my dear, I'm here!" I took her hand gently in mine. "I'm here. You are *awake,* and you are going to be *fine."*

"Something *caught,"* said Frances with great distress. "Waiting for Claire—so dark—rushed—something caught…"

"Darling, what caught? Who rushed? Rushed by? Rushed at you?" All eyes were riveted on Frances.

But at that moment her eyes closed, and once more she lost consciousness!

4 ✠ May 3

Frances is still out. How agonizing all this is! Just as we were about to learn something crucial, she left us again. I am still in New York, still sitting vigil by her bedside. But not all day long every day, for I've been to talk with Detective Pandolfo Morales, who was courteous but unable to give me details. Protocol. He said there were no firm leads at this point but that the investigation was of course very active. Then, on Sunday, I decided to attend the morning service at Saint Bede's and see whether I might talk with any clergy or choir members.

I arrived at 10:50 and slipped into a pew towards the front. Saint Bede's is a large, somewhat dark, old mock-Gothic structure, but with many attractive stained-glass windows with glinting royal blues and blood reds, images of Jesus, the saints, Old and New Testament characters. Old-fashioned heavy wooden pews with cranberry-colored cushions. An ample chancel with high altar and three rows of carved wooden choir stalls on each side, facing each other. Tall ornate wrought-iron stands supporting vases of fresh flowers. Impressive glittering chandeliers overhead. On the right side, a large pipe organ housed in a loft, its majestic rows of massive silver pipes spreading out to each side and soaring heavenwards. All what one might expect in a traditional Episcopal church, I suppose.

At 11:00 precisely, a little bell rang, we all stood, the organist began to play a stately hymn, and down the aisle marched a crucifer with towering bronze cross, two white-clad acolytes on either side bearing tall bright candles, Caspar dressed in his finery, followed by a similarly maroon-robed and white-surpliced choir of about twenty singers, another robed and surpliced man I assumed to be Averill Page, and at the end of the procession in single file, three members of the clergy in white cassocks and shiny green and gold floral-patterned chasubles. (Although Mother remained nominally Episcopalian right up until the end, bless her, when exactly was it that I'd last attended a regular church service? Christmas three years ago, I think it must have been, the midnight mass at Saint Peter's in Santa Maria.) Hymn, prayers, psalm, Old and New Testament readings, a measured sermon from the pulpit, the centuries-old creed, prayers and more prayers, an anthem by Mendelssohn which I recognized, communion, another anthem, a concluding hymn rounded out by yet more prayers (heavens, what have I forgotten to mention?), and there I was gathering up my jacket and bag with brain on fire as to how I might gain any insight at all into what had happened to my sister. Of course, during the service I looked carefully at the faces of each of the clergy, each of the singers. I thought I recognized the joyless, black-bespectacled face of Father Sauer, and perhaps I recognized two of the male singers Frances had mentioned in her emails, the tall blond tenor Vincent and the sturdy bass Victor.

I decided I'd join the reception line and shake hands with the priests. Two of them had positioned themselves along the side aisles, and I hoped it would be the rector who remained in my path, in the center aisle, whose name, I'd seen in the leaflet, was Father August Bakewell. When my turn arrived, I looked up into the face of a thin, kindly, older man, balding and brown-eyed, who wished me a good morning, even though the time was then 12:15. "Welcome," he added warmly. "Thank you," I said softly, adding, "I am Frances Whitestone's sister, Phoebe Overbridge, from California." His eyes widened and he put a bony hand to my shoulder. "I will be happy to talk with you in just a few minutes. Please don't go." I nodded and continued forward, walking slowly to the entrance of the church, where tables offered stacks of various pamphlets and leaflets.

Within ten minutes, his greeting duties concluded, I saw the long lean cassocked form of the rector gliding toward me down the center aisle. "I am Father August Bakewell, the rector of Saint Bede's," he said drawing next to me, his weighty-looking chasuble slung over one arm. "Please, come back to my office," and I followed him round the side of the nave and out a side door *(Ah, this must be the south door that the singers use!* came the realization), down two steps, along a path to a green courtyard, and arriving at a pretty little rectory with a patch of flowers embellishing each side of the front door. "My office parlor is right at the front. Please come in and I'll bring you a cup of tea."

Just before we entered, two figures hurriedly caught up with us, and the one in clerical dress said, "August, Victor has pointed out something that has been on my mind lately, too—just a quick word."

Father Bakewell, nodding, said, "Father Sauer, Victor, this is Phoebe Overbridge, Frances's sister." To me he added, "Victor Boindon is one of our excellent professional basses." As I murmured hello, each of the men displayed suitably chastened facial expressions. Victor is a tall, handsome, muscular man with sandy brown hair who appears to be in his mid-forties. Father Sauer is on the short side for a man, rather rotund in form but with very erect posture, somewhere in his fifties, with a head of carefully combed salt-and-pepper hair cut moderately short, and thick-framed black glasses.

Father Sauer said, "We are devastated, sorry beyond words, and hardly able to function these days. Thank God Frances did not suffer the same fate as Claire. It is all terrible, terrible. How is Frances doing?"

Deciding not to reveal Frances's brief surfacing into the light of a few days ago, I simply said, "She is still unconscious. We're…shattered."

Everyone looked down and remained silent for a moment, and then Father Sauer continued. "I see you were just going in to talk privately. I'll let you be. August, we just wanted to point out that there is a nasty unevenness in one of the stones along the center aisle, and several of the singers have mentioned almost tripping on it while processing and recessing. We really must call someone about that."

"Very true," said Father Bakewell. "I will have Everild deal with it. Thank you."

Once seated in a little front parlor office alone with Father Bakewell, a cup of Earl Grey tea steaming at my side, I looked deeply into the kindly and slightly cloudy eyes of this lean Episcopalian rector and decided it would be best to speak as frankly as possible. I told him that Frances had written to me a lot about how enjoyable singing in the chorus was, how she admired Caspar, Doug, and Averill, that I knew that the alto Claire had been identified as the woman found dead on the church grounds, and how Caspar had kindly called round the hospital after Frances. He listened patiently, one hand to his chin, nodding from time to time, occasionally looking down sadly at the large mock-Persian carpet that covered most of the parlor floor.

Finally I asked, "Do you have any idea what is behind all this?"

Father Bakewell shook his head sorrowfully, lifted both hands in the air to his sides, and said, "Not a clue. Nothing like this has ever happened here at Saint Bede's in the history of the place. We are cooperating fully with the police"—and here I mentioned that I'd spoken briefly with Detective Pandolfo Morales, who had revealed nothing to me—"but so far, we are as mystified as can be. We have always felt that Saint Bede's was a very warm, caring, and safe place for all. And of course all people, *any and all,* are welcome here."

"Do you know the choir members well, Father Bakewell?"

"No, I can't say I do. Most of them leave directly after the services."

"What about Averill, Doug, and Caspar?"

"Lovely men, all. Averill Page is a brilliant musician, as you may know, world-class organist and choral conductor. He came to us from a large Boston church about seven years ago. Young Doug Brinte, equally brilliant organist, a Royal Academy of Music grad, has been with us for about four years. Caspar Lang is Averill's student at the esteemed Breconford Academy of Music, a delightful young man from Connecticut, diligent and pleasant. I could not be happier with our music staff." I smiled and nodded respectfully. He went on. "Father Martyn Blum, our pastoral care priest, has been here as long as I, about, oh, twenty years now. It was he who discovered Frances that night…"

"Yes, Caspar told me."

"Thank God he'd left something in the church."

"Absolutely."

"And Father Radcliffe Sauer has been here for, let me see, about two years now, also from Boston, a hard-working man, specializes in planning the liturgy."

"Crazy, I know," I said, "to think any of the staff or singers here could have had anything to do with Claire's death or Frances's terrible fall."

"It must have been an intruder," pronounced Father Bakewell firmly. "That is our current thinking. Someone intent on theft, who may have struck or pushed each of the women aside as he was leaving the grounds. Detective Morales has told me that they believe Claire died of a blow to the head."

"Oh!" I exclaimed. "How hideous. Poor Claire. Frances mentioned her from time to time in her emails. Apparently the two were similar in appearance, same height, long black hair."

Father Bakewell responded with a somewhat benignly blank face, and I intuited that his powers of observation were not often directed to the appearance of the chorus members. I also realized that he was probably too removed from the personal lives of the Saint Bede's singers to be of much help in determining whether any romantic rivalries or hostilities might have played any part in the current tragedies. I therefore concluded our conversation as quickly as I could.

"Thank you so much, Father Bakewell, for taking the time to talk with me. I won't keep you any longer, but if you hear anything—"

"Of course, my dear. Never fear: we *will* get to the bottom of all this. Claire's death and Frances's grave injury are terrible sorrows for us all here at Saint Bede's, and we want all this cleared up and the guilty party—or parties—found just as much as you do, rest assured."

As Father Bakewell and I rose from our chairs, I saw him falter briefly and grab at the arm of the chair.

"Are you all right, sir?" I asked with some alarm.

"Fine, my dear. It's just my left hip. Or rather something around my hip, a muscle, a ligament, an unhappy piece of my anatomy. I've had it for years. It is an on-and-off phenomenon, rather irritatingly unpredictable."

"Have you had it checked?"

"Oh, yes. Many years ago I went to several different doctors, different specialists, you know, none of whom could pinpoint exactly what the source of pain was."

"How about an MRI?"

Father Bakewell smiled sagely, now fully erect, and replied, "Yes, dear, I've had those, too, years ago. But nothing showed up. It's my *phantom injury,* as I call it. Or perhaps some subtle yet admittedly aggravating repayment for a past sin, no doubt merited."

"I am no doctor, Father Bakewell, but I would think that perhaps another MRI might be in order, since your pain has only persisted over time?"

"I have thought of that, Phoebe. But you know—or perhaps you *don't,* lucky thing, so much younger than I, after all!—this would first require a new physical exam, and in my experience these exams themselves can cause a fair bit of suffering, as they push and pull you in various directions to try to 'elicit the pain source,' as they say, and at my ancient age, seventy-one, I am just that bit worried that a new exam could actually cause more lasting injury! And there is this aspect too: when the doctors don't know what the problem actually is, they suggest this, that, and the other thing. You may be surprised to know that an old relic like me has tried not only physical therapy but also acupuncture, reiki, homeopathic herbs, and a form of massage called the Bowen technique—I believe it is now somewhat popular in Australia, which is where I first heard of it. But none of these helped, and in fact sometimes I felt they aggravated the pain."

"Goodness. I am truly sorry to hear all this."

"Don't be, my dear. Even the blessed Paul apparently had a vexing pain in the side which God, in his at times inscrutable yet infallible wisdom, deigned not to eradicate. 'My grace is sufficient for thee,' as I recall. My haunch pain is minimal in the Grand Scheme of things, and I am profoundly grateful that it is not worse."

"That is a very philosophical approach, I must say."

"It is the only viable approach. And I must add, Phoebe, that you are kind to take an interest in this aspect of my old life, a subject I rarely even mention any more, for who is interested in the aches and pains of a withered old man?" I smiled warmly and tilted my head in sympathy, and to my surprise, he carried on. "One doctor I saw hinted at a possible surgery, but without a definite diagnosis, how could I submit to that? It could turn out disastrously! No, my *modus operandi* now is to carry on with a small amount of pharmaceutical assistance, for which I am thankful, and to await that inevitable moment of breakage, collapse"—my eyebrows shot up as I emitted a little gasp—"at which point I will indeed submit to another exam, an MRI, a CT scan, whatever is in vogue at that time, for surely *then,* whatever my point of weakness has been will be fully revealed."

I nodded and found myself smiling with appreciation at the aged Father Bakewell, who stood before me with such unexpected equanimity and cheerfulness.

"You are wise, sir," I said softly. "I do believe you have found exactly the right approach. And I wish you the very best."

*

After I left the leafy grounds of Saint Bede's to head back to the hospital, I stopped in to the French café just across the avenue, the Café Lyonnais, to order a take-out coffee. And there towards the back at a small round table with two young women was the bass Victor Boindon. Seeing me at the front counter, he excused himself from his companions and came to talk with me.

"Phoebe—we just met, you know, I'm Victor."

"Yes, hello," I murmured.

"I just wanted to say that I am devastated by what happened to Frances, and to Claire."

"Thank you."

"And…I don't know what Father Bakewell told you, but I can tell you that lately we've had a lot of tension in the music program there. It's not a rose garden, as he may have led you to believe."

"Oh!"

"Yes, you ought to know. I'd be happy to meet you for a talk, if you'd like."

"Well, yes, of course! When could that be?"

"I'm with a couple of the singers now, but could you meet me around 5:30 this afternoon? Not here, but say, somewhere off the beaten track, mid-town maybe?"

"Yes—you tell me where. I'll meet you."

So Victor suggested a pub on West 47th Street called the Old Goat.

*

Seated at a little high table along the wall, back and away from the bar, Victor and I settled in with tall glasses of old English hard cider.

"Cheers."

"Cheers."

"Except that there is not much to be cheerful about just now," said Victor, and I agreed. "I want to tell you first that we all love Frances. She is a spark of positive energy at Saint Bede's." I smiled warmly and he continued. "We don't rehearse with the chorus—there are actually three choirs there, the kids, the community chorus, and the professional choir."

"Yes, Frances has told me."

"Right. Well, I'm a pro and we see the chorus only on those Sundays when we all combine to sing a service. The kids sing about twice a month, one morning and one evening service; the chorus a little more often. The three groups have never actually been introduced to each other, but over time, well, you meet a few people, and you also recognize who the really good singers are. The community chorus is quite good and has a large mix of ages, and well, I just wanted to say that Frances does stand out: she has a lovely bell-like soprano voice."

"That's very nice to hear, thank you."

"Well, anyway," Victor continued, glancing to each side as he sighed deeply, "I wanted to let you know that although they are saying around church right now that whoever bashed up Claire and Frances must have been an intruder, the atmosphere lately, even before these horrible events, has been pretty miserable."

"Really! In what ways?"

"Oh gosh, you name it! Father Sauer, who's been with us about two years now, has slowly but surely been trying to make the place more 'high church,' as they say. You know—smells, bells, Rite I liturgy, more formal, more sort of Catholic in feel. He's what you would call *uptight* in lots of ways, seems to me the stereotypical repressed introverted cleric living in his head. He wants more very traditional church music, more plainchant, very old hymns, Renaissance masses. Nothing expressly wrong with that, I suppose, some very good stuff there. But Averill, the music director, is more in favor of a *via moderna,* if you like, prefers Rite II, likes trying new pieces, sometimes jazzy ones, in fact, and even really gutsy black spiritual arrangements. So over the past two years, we singers have overheard some pretty heated conversations—of course we're not meant to hear them, but we do, and then of course everyone talks about them and the various issues, and singers even take sides. Parish life. Peace, love, joy, covert sniping and insults—ha, ha, the church, you know."

"I have to admit that although our family still calls itself Episcopalian, Frances is the only one at this point who actively participates in the church."

"My father is actually an atheist, which I think is taking things a bit far," said Victor. "He believes, and will let you know in no uncertain terms, that organized religions contribute nothing to the world but superstition, intolerance, war, and death. The Irish Protestants and Catholics—the Sunnis and the Shias—the Israeli Jews and the Palestinian Muslims—well, he does have a point! For me, well, all religions at their best teach love, justice, truth, compassion—the highest human values—but—don't mean to be getting off the track here—I personally am at Saint Bede's mainly to *sing!*"

"Music soothes the savage beast in all of us," I remarked.

"Indeed it does," Victor agreed, pausing for a long drink of cider. "But going on. Within our pro choir, more bad feelings have recently reared up because although we are all soloists, Averill has been choosing the same singers for solo lines for the past few weeks, and that rankles. We all took this job thinking we'd each in turn get to sing solo sections, but it's not turning out that way. So the green-eyed monster rears up—jealousy, envy. Jockeying for Averill's attention. That sort of thing. Very tedious, makes for bad vibes. I don't much mind whatever line I'm given—I sing with two other groups, including a new small opera company that we're just now getting off the ground, quite exciting."

I nodded appreciatively. He went on. "As for the chorus, as I said, I don't know many of them, but I was getting to know Claire, in fact, such a lovely person! She was from Montreal, bilingual in English and French, of course, and incredibly smart." Here he frowned and shook his head. "I'm so angry—who on earth would want to harm her? It makes no sense at all. Or Frances!"

"It's appalling," I said.

Victor finished off his cider and gestured to the barman for another.

"Well, a few days before Claire was…before she died—I mean, who knows what happened—I was going to say 'killed' because a woman of her age doesn't just drop down dead at the foot of a piano, does she? But the police will figure all that out—I hope. Well, about a week before, I'd asked her out for the second time, and as we were talking over dinner she mentioned that some long-time chorus members were starting to feel that they were treated as second-class citizens at Saint Bede's."

"How exactly?"

"Not given the best pieces to sing, for example. Many of them have been choral singers for years, in other groups, and have performed the great stuff from the choral repertoire. But at Saint Bede's, it's true, the chorus is given the rather easy anthems to perform, and it's us, the pro choir, who get to sing Byrd, Monteverdi, Bach, Britten, the more challenging and, you'd have to say, interesting pieces. So Claire told me a bit of grumbling was going on among chorus members."

"I see."

"Then, at the end of the academic year, in very early May, the chorus sings their last service—"

"They don't sing during the summer?"

"No. The kids' choir goes on for another two weeks, and the pros sing all summer, but the chorus stops in early May. Some chorus members feel a bit short shrifted that way, but another point is this. They are all volunteers, you know. Claire was saying that each May, an end-of-year party is organized for the chorus, *by* the chorus—where they all bring dishes for a potluck. The clergy don't even treat them to a paid meal in a pizzeria, which they do for us, the pro choir, each December. And the lady who takes care of the kids, the den-mother Caroline, who happens to be a chorus alto: she puts in hours and hours chaperoning the kids on a strictly volunteer basis. They pay her nothing, not even a Christmas gift certificate!

"Wow."

"So you see, alack and alas, a lot more beneath the surface of the angelic voices you hear at our services!"

"I'm getting it." I took a long drink of my cider and then asked, "Caspar and Doug, are they well liked? Caspar actually came to visit Frances the other day at the hospital."

"They are fantastic. Nice guys, hard-working. Doug is a genius, a world-class organist from London, and he's been given more and more conducting responsibilities over the past couple of years and works really well with us. He's a star, for sure. Caspar is fairly new, really warm and friendly, as you probably noticed. And very good looking! The dashing young bachelor."

I smiled and said, "Frances has commented on that in her emails to me. She loves describing everything about her chorus experiences. I would reckon that Caspar is pretty well sought-after there."

"For sure! The sopranos and altos flirt with him—and a couple of the tenors, too! The jury is still out on whether he might be gay…"

"I think he's straight," I said. "Caspar and I had a long talk in the hospital cafeteria when he came to visit, and he made that pretty clear. But I see how his looks could cause confusion."

"Oh, good to know," said Victor with slightly raised eyebrows. "Averill thinks the world of him—you know Averill is gay, right?"

"Yes."

"Caspar is Averill's conducting student at Breconford. Averill, as you probably know, leads major choirs and orchestras here in town, and lately he's had Caspar come along to video them and to help out generally pre- and post-performances. I was the bass soloist with Averill's *Messiah* last December, and afterwards the soloists, a couple of the instrumentalists, Averill, and Caspar all went out for drinks. I sat across the table from Averill and Caspar, who were seated side by side, and I noticed Averill directing a lot of doting attention on Caspar, hand to his shoulder, taps to his hand, that sort of thing. They both can throw them back, too!"

I smiled with slightly raised eyebrows.

"I shouldn't say that," said Victor looking a bit sheepish. "But it's true. But then many conductors do this to relax after big performances, and quite a few singers, too."

"It's quite understandable, doesn't bother me," I said. "And after all that effort and all the joy and excitement they've brought to their audiences—well, they deserve to celebrate."

"You're right. Caspar did say a few things in the course of that conversation that made it clear that he's out pretty often with Averill for drinks—after class, too, it seems."

During a moment of silent reflection, I recalled something my darling Matt had suggested on the phone the other evening, that maybe Averill had grown possessive of Caspar in more than one way and felt resentful of the fond friendship he perceived developing between Caspar and Frances. I pondered again various occasions that Frances had related in her emails of what could be considered outright bantering flirtation between herself and Caspar. So, mentioning none of this but deciding to be cautiously frank, I asked, "Do you think Averill is attracted to Caspar?"

"Well, yes. For sure he is. But then everyone is attracted to Caspar!"

I smiled. "Ah, to be young and beautiful—youth is precious! Do you think there is competition also for Caspar's attention among the pros and the chorus?"

Victor pondered a moment. "Maybe. It's always in the first couple of months after someone new arrives that things feel a bit tense and fluid—you know, everyone wondering who this dashing person is going to pair up with. But Caspar's been with us now since September, and apparently he's not going out with any of the singers. We pros, except for one or two, are all a bit older than he is, and many of the chorus singers are *quite* a bit older, you know, fifties right up to eighties! A couple young students there, too, of course. Caspar makes no secret also that he is Roman Catholic and very pious. He's also pretty attached to his mother. She comes to almost all his services, and we see him embracing her before and afterwards!"

"A good mama's boy?"

"You could probably say that," Victor agreed, chuckling. "I think his mother is from Mexico—you know those possessive Latin mothers, they adore their sons, probably spoil them rotten! But in any case, since Caspar is only the assistant choirmaster and still a student, there is no jockeying for his attention in the sense that any of us pros feel we really have any professional advantages to gain from him."

"That makes sense."

"There's one more thing I should tell you," Victor went on. "The church office staff these past months has been like a merry-go-round.

Everild is fiercely loyal to the rector—you know, the stereotypical passionately ascetic and devoted church secretary type—and she is like the Rock of Gibraltar at Saint Bede's. But various assistants have come and gone, apparently with some acrimonious feelings."

"Why is that?"

"No one is quite sure, and we like Everild, but she can be rather bossy, word has it. For those of us who interact only briefly with her, it's hard to see the big picture. But one assistant, Lucy, who recently left, who was in charge of coordinating student data for the school—you know Saint Bede's has a small school attached, K to 8, private, rather posh—told one of the pros, whom she was meeting for coffee occasionally, that she couldn't stand Everild, found her a micro-manager and a bit demeaning to boot. Everild dresses very conservatively, and Lucy was only about twenty-five and tended to wear rather tight jeans and tight, brightly colored sweaters—Everild gave her a hard time about that, we heard. Lucy stayed only about four months and then quit—or was fired, we're not sure which. Another assistant, a young guy, Trevor, who specifically worked for Averill and the music program, also stayed only about six months and then quit. He was only part-time and a singer himself—not with us, but in various groups in town—and I'd heard complaints from some of our parishioners who contribute to the music program that their checks tended to take a long time to show as cleared." I nodded and recalled Frances's story of her lost check, finally located in Caspar's Mozart score, but again I said nothing. "My neighbor, in fact," Victor went on, "is a contributor and loves to come hear us sing on Sundays, and he told me he'd had to call on two different occasions, around Christmas time and Easter time, to check on why his donations had still not cleared with his bank. Apparently, Trevor slotted the checks into some little nook or cranny and only went to deposit them maybe every three or four weeks. Lazy."

"Not nice," I agreed. "Not respectful to the donors, is it."

"No." Victor finished off his second cider, rolled his broad shoulders a few times, glanced quickly to the side, and stretched his arms wide. It was now after 6:45, more thirsty people were wandering in, and the Old Goat barman had jacked up the volume on the new-age-rock-Irish music he was piping out to the establishment. "Anyway," Victor went on, "there you have it. I just wanted to let you know that Saint Bede's is not exactly as it may appear, a serene and harmonious flowery Episcopal haven in west Harlem. Things are stewing there, pretty much all the time."

"I really, really appreciate your telling me all this, Victor. I sincerely do. Maybe somebody got angry about something, an argument broke out, someone shoved the two women… Although, goodness, I'm still not at all sure what if anything either of those women had to do with any church problems."

"Nothing," said Victor. "I can't see it. Lovely women, both. But maybe caught at the wrong place at the wrong time?"

"Maybe. Hmm…"

"Well, I ought to go now, but we can talk again if you want, if anything more comes up."

"That is great of you, Victor, thank you. I'll let you know. For now, I'm just visiting Frances every day, praying she will wake up."

"We're all praying for her," said Victor, patting my hand as we stood to exit the bar.

*

Back at the hospital, I checked in first with the nurses' station, and Violet told me Frances had remained sleeping the entire day. Once more seated in her room with a take-out box of chicken curry and vegetables on my lap that I'd picked up from the corner market, I gazed at Frances's sleeping form. As I bit slowly into a limp green bean, I glanced up at the clear bag of liquid nutrition hanging on a pole that was, via an intravenous line inserted into Frances's left forearm, keeping my sister alive. I felt bone-crushingly tired after the long day out, the two intense conversations, and the ear-shattering trajectories in the New York City subway to and from the Old Goat. Most of all, I felt a long way from having any key insights into what might have led to the utter sorrow that was now facing me.

After I finished my dinner, I decided to scroll through more of Frances's emails to me.

*

March 20

Dear Phoebe,

Rehearsals for Easter are ramping up in intensity, as you might imagine, the guys working us hard, and I'm pleased that I seem to have made a place for myself there as one of the strongest sopranos. You know the fun Caspar and I tend to have, and now he's taken to asking me questions rather regularly about various things. "Frances, the Brahms score—what number is that?" (For an alto had been away and come back and needed a copy.) "Everybody, I believe last time we shortened that quarter note to an eighth for a quick breath—Frances, am I right, do you have that marked?" That sort of thing. Warms my old heart! Caspar really is such a nice young man, and it would be sweet if we could be friends, but of course we can't be, not really. If he could consider me an auntie or just a platonic friend, then I think it could work! For we do seem to have some warm, genuine connection—frankly, I think we are a bit attracted to each other!—but of course many various obstacles stare me in the face, and I feel some tension. Maybe simple friendship is never actually possible between men and women who are within twenty years of each other's age—maybe nature just doesn't allow that. (Manipulative, powerful Mother Nature: so intent on pressing every species into reproducing itself, by hook or by crook! It's all hormones, isn't it!) I've found myself thinking about Caspar more and more outside of rehearsals, and I realize that I need to "act my age," if you like, and not let the excitement of being around this comely youth delude me. Fun it may be, but possible it is not.

So for the past couple of meetings—church and rehearsal—as I've arrived I've made a point not *to seek out Caspar or make eye contact, just to behave as a neutral, happy chorus member. Chatting with other singers is a good way to do this. Last Sunday, chorus was on for evensong and I was doing well with my new more sagacious approach, when this happened. The chorus had had a quick warm-up in the basement hall with Doug and Caspar, and then Averill and the pros joined us for the final run-through of the service's pieces. We then all dispersed back to our robing rooms—each group has its own, also in the basement. After I'd put on my robe and surplice and filled my water bottle, I was standing chatting with a fellow soprano, singers milling and talking on all sides. It was time for us all to go up, and for this service we were not processing, just going straight to our places in the choir stalls. As I began to move forward, there was Caspar looking my way, and although I made a sort of attempt to maneuver away around some singers, he came straight to me and gave me a big hug! Well! The crowd of singers continued exiting the hall towards the corridor and stairs up to the chancel, but Caspar and I stood rooted to the spot for a moment, asking each other how we were. Fine. Fine. He actually looked a bit thin to me, probably the effects of his Lenten fasting.*

"How is Mom?" I asked.

"She's in the hospital."

"Oh no! What happened?"

"You know she sprained her ankle and has been wearing that boot. Well, the pain wasn't going away and she was starting to run a fever, and so yesterday we drove her back to the hospital. When they took the boot and taping off, they saw that her foot and ankle were very red and swollen—they sent her straight over for an MRI, and it's not just a sprain, it's a fracture! A fracture in her fibula, and an infection on top of that."

"Oh, goodness!" I exclaimed. "Awful. I just hate stories like that! Stupid doctors! You know, x-rays miss a lot—happened to me once with a wobbly tooth. I went in complaining of it, and the dentist x-rayed, it: 'Fine, A-OK.' Two days later, half the tooth cracked off! Anyway, so they are keeping her at the hospital for a while now?"

"Yes, because of the infection—it had started to spread. She'll be on IV antibiotics I think for a week or two."

"Poor thing. I was in that situation once, years ago. Hooked up to the line and little plastic bags. Not fun. I'm really sorry to hear this, Caspar."

Caspar darted over to the water fountain, and I just stood where I was. By that time all of the other singers had left the hall, and we needed to go, too. "I'll walk in with you," said Caspar.

As we walked, he confided softly that he was wondering whether he should go live at home for a while to help his mother once she was discharged from the hospital, since his father was at work all day. "Maybe," I responded. "You will never regret helping your parents. I had to go stay with my dear old dad once after he'd had surgery—he was living alone—my mother had died long before. I was very glad I went to help him. You've got only one set of parents in this life."

"So true."

When we got up to the choir stalls, all the singers, choir and chorus, were seated, with Averill standing at the conducting stand in position to begin, and Caspar and I were rather conspicuous, entering late together. I saw a few alto and soprano eyes dart my way. Averill looked at Caspar and me a moment longer than necessary and a very small smile played around his lips. Father Sauer, who appeared to be the priest in charge of this service, also looked my way, sporting his tight little grimace. I took my seat in the chorus soprano section and Caspar went to sit with the basses, and the service began.

Afterwards, after disrobing and shelving my Stanford Magnificat *and* Nunc Dimittis, *I did not seek out Caspar but left promptly, not wanting to change my well-thought-out* modus operandi. *Still, I felt warm and happy inside. I felt very moved that Caspar had wanted to talk with me, had in fact sought me out for that hug and quick conversation. And having to speak quite softly, as we had done, was also rather comforting somehow, as Caspar and I have a similar sort of timbre to our voices. Maybe, I thought to myself, we are becoming genuine friends. Of a sort.*

All for now.

Love, Frances

*

March 29

Dear Phoebe,

Just to fill you in a bit more: I adored the five-day trip to Mexico! I'm glad you liked my photos. Mérida is a little dream city, so very Spanish colonial, flowers in all the public plazas, lots of beautiful old architecture, and the weather perfectly warm and sunny. A perfect late-winter getaway. As you saw, we made several excursions to various Mayan temples from there, and I felt really invigorated climbing some of those tall pyramids! As they told us to do, I assiduously avoided the tap water and any raw fruits or veg that could have been washed in tap water. A few others of our small group came down with the dreaded Mayan Tummy—they said their error must have been to drink a beverage in a café with ice. Ice made of tap water. E. coli, horrible! Bottled water all the way, you know, plastic upon plastic. Really, I think Mexico desperately needs to invest in a country-wide water purification system! But otherwise, public-health infrastructure aside, I do love Mexico, and the local people were so friendly. Maybe I will retire in the Yucatán when I hit sixty-two or so!

In chorus news, I was happy to get back to rehearsal last night. Doug was very pleased with the sopranos, and sure enough I noticed that I was rather the section leader. Nice to feel needed. Same rehearsal leadership pattern that I had noticed before Mexico: Doug is doing the overwhelming amount of conducting, with Caspar currently in charge of only two rather easy pieces, with Doug accompanying on the piano. You see, when Doug leads, he conducts and plays because he is a virtuoso organist and phenomenal sight-reader. I hope Caspar is okay with this, maybe realizing that he in turn is the head honcho with the kids' choir—division of labor sort of thing. Caspar I am sure realizes, sadly, his weakness on the keyboard.

After rehearsal people cleared out remarkably fast—we had rehearsed until 9:30, thirty minutes longer than usual, because the previous rehearsal had been cancelled owing to a snow storm. Suddenly, the only people left in the room were Doug, Caroline (alto, and the kids' chaperone), Caspar, and I. Doug went to confer with Caroline about something, and I quietly asked Caspar whether his mother was still in the hospital or now back at home. Hopefully going home very soon, he said, adding that his sister and her family had just driven down to visit her. He showed me a phone photo of his sister, her husband, and their adorable little daughter. "Please give your mother my best," I said, "and tell her I miss chatting with her after the services." Saying he would, since he spoke with her daily on the phone, Caspar proceeded to take a short turn around the hall.

As I was donning scarf, coat, and hat, Caspar returned to stand closer to me, and feeling so moved, I reached for a little high-bouncing rubber ball in my bag, saying, "Caspar, I have a present for you!" I extracted an exquisite little green marbled one and said, tossing it in the air, "See this?" He was immediately intrigued. "Ready? Catch!" and I tossed it up a few inches towards him.

He caught it eagerly, bounced it, and smiled broadly. "A high-bounce ball!" he exclaimed. "For my niece?" Doug and Caroline smiled, and Caroline waved good-bye as she exited the hall. Doug moved to file away sheet music in boxes behind the piano.

"Or whatever," I replied pleasantly. "For hand-eye coordination, or muscle-therapy ball."

He walked all around the hall, bouncing it and throwing it up in the air with abandon.

"I got a pack of twelve."

"In Mexico?"

"Yes, just for fun." (Actually, I'd thought they would be useful as little muscle massage balls for my aging back!)

He was clearly enjoying himself, bouncing the green ball repeatedly as Doug looked on with amusement. Caspar said, "You could drop this from a really tall height and see how far it comes back up."

"Don't do that," I replied, and we all three laughed.

Caspar observed, "This could do a lot of damage in a small room…"

I shook my head, smiling.

"Maybe I won't give it to my niece, too much fun. I may not get much studying done tonight!"

I felt secretly delighted to have unleashed the little boy in him! I turned my mind to the fact that I needed a ladies room trip before heading home, and I confirmed that if when I came out everything was all locked up, I could still get out of the church. "Oh yes," confirmed both Doug and Caspar. But when I came out of the restroom, Caspar was right in that ante-space linking the hall, the robing rooms, the acolyte room, and the restrooms, and he was bouncing the magical green ball right up to the high ceiling, completely enthralled with his new toy. I laughed with glee and smiled broadly at him, tilting my head, and he tilted his head, too, and smiled back. A lovely moment! I'd wanted something to de-stress him from the worry over his mother, and nothing could have served better than that little high-bounce ball!

"It's fun, isn't it?" I remarked. "I'm enjoying mine."

And before I left, I looked back and added, "Green: our beautiful globe!" I use that expression "our beautiful globe" a lot when I share photos. "Okay, bye, see you!" I said finally, heading for the door, with Caspar's joyful face emblazoned in my mind's eye. How tickled I felt!

Once home, I found myself staying up very late to watch a movie, Suddenly, Last Summer, *which tells of the strange, obsessive, and basically emotionally if not physically incestuous passion of a mother (Katherine Hepburn) for her beloved "poet" son Sebastian (Montgomery Clift), and his tragic end in a foreign country (Mexico?) while traveling with his fresh young cousin (Elizabeth Taylor). Fascinating film! Turns out, as I'd foreseen, that it is not the cousin who is insane or unbalanced but rather the mother, unable to face the truth about her narcissistic son and his violent end. Mothers and sons: now* there *is a recurring theme in literature, no? I suddenly wondered whether Caspar felt at all oppressed by his adoring mother! What was it that William Somerset Maugham remarked in this vein… I shall Google it. "Few misfortunes can befall a boy which bring worse consequences than to have a really affectionate mother."*

Phoebe, my dear, I've rambled on far too long as usual, but it seems I've become very interested in the close observation of our delightful assistant choirmaster and his family! It makes for an engrossing project.

Please give Matt my best, and very sorry to hear about his slight relapse with the shoulder. Tell him that Frances says: "Dear Matt, although your soul is immortal, your earthly body is not, so please go easy!!" Will he at last be convinced to cease lifting heavy boxes and leave that to his younger team? Men.

F. xo

5 ✠ May 6

The time drags on… Today, after seeing no progress with my dear Frances and feeling nearly at wits' end, I decided I would try to speak with more staff at Saint Bede's. I called the church office and spoke with Everild Dunne—she does sound as punctilious and efficient as I've been led to believe. I asked whether Averill Page was available to talk. She put me on hold for a couple of minutes, then returned to say no, he was in fact about to fly out for a performing engagement in Germany, Messiaen organ works at the cathedral in Cologne, gone a total of five days. I then asked whether the pastoral care priest, Father Blum, was there. Again put on hold, but the next voice I heard said, "This is Father Blum. How can I help you?" He agreed to speak with me privately, and at 11:00, there I was, once more on the flowery grounds of Saint Bede's, this time in the small consulting room of the priest in charge of counseling troubled souls. I was definitely one of these. Father Blum settled into his chair, comfortably erect, a man of medium height and chubby form, with pleasant, pale-blue eyes, a straight nose, and a full head of grey wavy hair.

He was dressed in clerical black with crisp white collar. He looked to be in his late-sixties.

With a cup of chamomile tea steaming on the little table at my side, I began. "Father Blum, thank you for meeting with me, very kind."

"Of course, Mrs. Overbridge."

"As you can imagine, I am terribly frustrated at this point. My sister is still lying unconscious in the hospital, and it seems the police have made no progress in figuring any of this horror out. Have you heard anything?"

"I understand your distress, of course, and I am moved that you are continuing to sit vigil at her bedside. We feel devastated here, as you must realize. The short answer to your question is: *Not a great deal.* But yesterday afternoon Father Bakewell got a call from the police that a neighborhood man had been taken in for questioning. Someone apparently saw him lurking around the church in the evening on the days prior to the incidents."

"Oh! Do you know who he is?"

"I was actually called in, briefly, to the precinct when they first brought him in, as he asked for a priest. I sat with him privately in the holding area before he was questioned by the police, and of course that conversation must remain confidential. But I can tell you simply that I did recognize the man as one who comes fairly regularly for meals at our Saturday soup kitchen in the basement hall, and who also often attends the main Sunday service. He is a curious, unfortunate soul. He was a high-school mathematics teacher for ten years in the Bronx. Quite handsome, well built. One day after a private catch-up tutoring session in algebra, he told me, the young female pupil he was helping went to the police and accused him of sexual misconduct with her. Inquiries were made at the school with the principal and so forth, and the man—his name is Craig Scranch—vehemently denied the charges. He said the girl had shown signs of a crush on him, had often asked for after-school help, but when he'd made it definitively clear that it was *math only,* she became infuriated, feeling rebuffed. According to Craig, out of anger and spite she then made the accusation against him."

"Hell hath no fury like a woman scorned," I mused. "I mean, if that was the case."

"The girl eventually dropped the charge, in fact, but not before basically ruining Craig's teaching career and possibly his life. He has not been able to find full-time work since that incident, which happened about a year ago. He relies on our Saturday kitchen and a few others round town to stay adequately fed. It's a sad story. We clergy here have observed him now for months, without much conversation, as he keeps mostly to himself. I pop into the Saturday kitchen from time to time, and I see him always sitting slightly apart from the others, eating quietly alone. You know, we try to make all people welcome at Saint Bede's, no matter what their status in life, but we don't pry. Of course we are available to talk if people come to us, but otherwise we just adopt a policy of 'live and let live.'"

"I see, yes. Poor Craig Scranch. Still, do you have any feeling about whether he was the sort of man capable of attacking women—in this case, Claire and Frances? And would he have had a reason to do that?"

"Anger at women in general, you mean? I would say I very much doubt it. He probably has great resentment still from the injustice he suffered from that pupil's false accusation, but I don't sense a violent temperament in him at all. I've seen him in the pews sitting mid-way back all the way to the left side on Sunday mornings, his facial expression more sad than angry. He does not take communion, but he seems to find some comfort from our services. I have noticed him talking afterwards to other congregants only very rarely, never with the singers—he usually leaves immediately. As I said, I had a private conversation with him yesterday, which I cannot describe to you, but I am hoping for the best. I am not sure whether the police are still holding him or not."

"Okay," I murmured, feeling as disappointed as ever with the glacial pace at which progress was being made in solving these crimes. So I decided to ask some hard questions as tactfully as I could. "Father Blum, since you are the pastoral care priest, you must have very good insight into people and their feelings, even though everyone of course tries to hide their deepest emotions. But you probably notice things others would not. What I mean is, well, although Saint Bede's seems a peaceful, pretty place, I know that nothing is ever quite what it appears." I was thinking of all that the bass Victor had shared with me but decided to remain mum about that. "Our mother—Frances's and my mother, may she rest in peace—used to attend church regularly, working with the altar guild arranging flowers and that kind of thing, and we were always entertained—forgive me!—by the many stories she brought home of in-fighting among church staff."

Father Blum's eyebrows rose slightly and he allowed a small smile to break across his pleasant face. "Men are fallible," he remarked. "That is no secret. And can be petty, and mentally flawed. Only God is perfect."

"Yes. Well, what I mean is, since apparently nothing has been stolen from the church, could it be that Claire's death and Frances's injury were the result of some hostility among people here? I'm very sorry to ask such a thing, but…well, for example, could there have been some romantic rivalry going on involving Claire and my sister?"

"Goodness. Hard questions. I hardly know what to reply. I know very little about the personal lives of the singers here."

I decided to probe more daringly. "I attended your Sunday service recently, as you may know, and Frances used to write to me in detail about all her experiences with the chorus. She loves it, by the way. I have noticed, if you will allow me to remark, that Father Sauer presents quite a severe, gloomy face, which accords with a few observations Frances has made. Is he…"

"Father Sauer, bless him," Father Blum interrupted, "is a most hard-working man. It is interesting, I have to say, that priests who specialize in liturgy do tend to have that severe look: I think they are critiquing the services carefully at every moment as they are unfolding. You know—are the leaflets error-free? Are the pauses between prayers long enough? Regarding the choirs: is the distance between the ranks of singers as they process in and out a consistent four feet, or are they straggling? Is their demeanor suitably serious and not frivolous? Is the women's hair properly pulled back and out of their faces? Our choir members here are a merry bunch, which I find quite delightful, but Father Sauer demands a staid decorum at every point in the services. He is a very detail-oriented man, our Father Sauer, and I suppose this is as it must be. But his look does tend to be severe. He never married—the church is his life."

I listened to this description with secret revulsion but tried to keep my facial expression neutral. I imagined Father Sauer as a lonely, pent-up obsessive-compulsive, secretly very attracted to women but socially inept and avowed to a strict, abstemious clerical life. Joy through the minutiae of the liturgy. Frustrated by his futile attraction to women. Claire and Frances, with their young pretty faces and long flowing dark hair, *Temptresses*…

"I'm sure all personality types can find their niche in the church," I murmured.

Father Blum's eyes narrowed very slightly, but he nodded and continued. "Father Sauer is harmless. He wouldn't hurt a fly. Actually, he does swat flies quite vigorously—summers here are very hot and humid, and thank the Lord we have at last installed new screens and more air conditioners in the clergy apartments—but people, no. He is very restrained, reclusive, a cordial man but not effusive by any means. We value his gifts here, and we tolerate what some may see as his…weaknesses."

"No doubt a sensible policy for life in general," I mused. "For dealing with everyone, I mean."

"Quite."

"Forgive me for one more question, Father Blum: was it you who came across Frances that night?"

"Who told you that?"

"Caspar mentioned it when he came to visit us at the hospital a few days ago."

"Yes, it was I. I can't tell you how upsetting that was, even for someone like me who is used to hearing about the never-ending vagaries of human confusion, misconduct, and sin. Listening to what people feel and may be capable of, and actually running across a *body* lying on the path are quite different experiences, I discovered that night."

"It must have been frightful!"

"Very much so. It was dark, of course, but we do have a few ground lights along that path. I recall one of them was out, now that I think about it. I was on my way back to the church to retrieve a book I'd left in the pulpit—I'd preached at a small wedding earlier that day. When I saw a collapsed figure along the path, I just stopped dead in my tracks—pardon me, poor choice of words!—and then turned back straight away to go to Father Bakewell at the rectory. He phoned the police immediately, of course, 911. We were both trembling."

"Yet Frances was not dead."

"Thankfully, but it appeared so, and I was so distraught that as I said, I went straight to the rectory. The police and an ambulance arrived within about four minutes."

"I got a call from the hospital where they took Frances at about 7:50 p.m. west-coast time—which is 10:50 here in New York—and I took a red-eye straight out, went immediately to the hospital when I arrived early in the morning."

Father Blum nodded.

"Then, I think it was that very morning, Friday, that Claire's body was found?"

"Yes. Horror upon horror. None of us clergy had got a wink of sleep that night, only to learn about Claire the next morning. We've never had anything like this happen at Saint Bede's!"

"Dr. Lasso told me about Claire only the following day, Saturday, although I didn't learn her name until a few days later."

Father Blum and I looked plaintively into each other's eyes. I saw real sorrow there, and pity and compassion.

"Father Blum, I won't take any more of your time. You've been very kind to talk with me. Is there anything else, anything at all, that comes to mind that could give any insight into what may have happened that night?"

He sighed, looked down at his pale, slightly wrinkled hands, shook his grey head gently, and replied, "I'm afraid I can't. I wish I could. I simply am just as confused and in the dark as everyone else here."

At that moment a rap came on the door, and Everild opened it and peered in discreetly. "Father Blum, the masonry man is here for the nave step repair, and Father Bakewell is out: could you spare a moment? I do apologize."

I said quickly, "I'll let you go, Father Blum. Thank you so much for talking with me. I'll be off."

"We'll be in touch as soon as anything becomes clearer, my dear, rest assured," said Father Blum rising slowly from his chair.

6 ✠ May 9

Sunday again, and again I decided to attend Saint Bede's. I arrived at 10:50 and as I scanned the congregation I saw, mid-way back all the way to the left, a dejected-looking man sitting alone, and I remembered Father Blum's story about the unfortunate former math teacher Craig Scranch. Not knowing exactly what I was after but hoping this man was he, I casually slid into the same pew and sat down near him. If this was indeed Craig, he'd clearly been released by the police and was no longer a suspect. Observing him as unobtrusively as I could during the service, and reaching out to shake his hand at the passing of the peace, I sensed he was an intelligent soul and might possibly have valuable insights about Saint Bede's in general. Although his countenance hinted at loneliness, his general appearance was pleasant, a very slim man somewhere in his mid-thirties, with unexpectedly deep-blue eyes and a face framed by medium-length light brown hair that had grown perhaps a tad too long. He wore a plain pale-blue collared shirt and jeans.

At the conclusion of the service, I scrambled mentally for the right way to broach a bit of conversation with him. Deciding on the simple and direct approach, I smiled and said, "Hello, I'm Phoebe."

He looked at me with slightly raised eyebrows, and I surmised that he was not used to being greeted in this way at Saint Bede's. But he quickly recovered a neutral yet agreeable look on his face and, to my great satisfaction, responded, "Hello. I'm Craig."

"I'm from out of town," I said. "This is only the second service I've attended here. Are you a long-time member?" I felt my attempts at conversation were feeble, but I had to start somewhere.

"About a year."

"A good church?"

He smiled enigmatically and looked away briefly before saying, "I don't really get involved. But the music is nice."

"Yes, it is." The notion quickly came to me that only the truth would serve and so I said, "I should tell you: I am Frances's sister, you know the soprano who was found injured here on the grounds recently."

Craig's eyes widened and his brow furrowed deeply, his face stricken with concern.

"Don't worry. She is hanging in there, still in the hospital, and there is every hope that she'll recover."

Craig remained silent. Then he said, "I've seen and heard things around this place that would raise the hair on your head."

My turn to be taken aback! "Oh really?"

"Things are never what they seem," he murmured.

"Craig, I would be very indebted to you to know what you've seen. May I invite you to lunch with me?"

*

Seated at a little Mexican restaurant several streets away from the church, waiting for our tacos and enchiladas, two bottles of Dos Equis on the table before us, I looked expectantly and nervously into Craig Scranch's crystal-blue eyes. This is what he had to say.

"I used to teach high-school math, algebra and geometry mostly. That all ended about a year ago when a mixed-up sophomore who was coming to me for tutoring accused me of coming on to her sexually. Totally untrue. A nightmare. She had a crush on me. I was used to students having crushes on me—pardon my frankness here, but it is what it is." I smiled understandingly and nodded in acknowledgement of his good looks. "Once during an algebra session I rather pointedly rebuffed her flirtations, and I think that really hurt and angered her—in fact, *unhinged* her, as the next morning she went to the principal and accused me of repeatedly trying to kiss her—*absurd."*

I grimaced and respectfully remained silent, wanting him to go on. He did.

"Well, to cut a long story short, as you can imagine, my life turned upside down. This nasty little blond nymph eventually dropped the charges, thank God, admitted she'd made the whole thing up, but by then I'd lost my job and no one in the city was willing to hire me."

"Very, very sorry to hear it," I said softly.

"Nightmare," he repeated. "Have you noticed that society has gone pretty haywire lately in a lot of disturbing ways? All a woman has to do now is accuse a man, a perfectly upright, hard-working professional, of misconduct, and *wham!* He's out on his ass. Guilty before proven innocent. Excuse me, but I'm still pretty angry about what happened."

"Understandably."

"Well, about three months ago I finally had to give up my apartment—savings ran out, couldn't afford it—and I moved into a single rented room here in the neighborhood. I've been doing a part-time job, barely keeping body and soul together—pathetic really, when you consider I have a degree from Rutgers."

"What kind of job?"

"Telephone tech assistance for laptops."

"Well, that's something useful."

"I'm still alive, you could say. I eat at the Saint Bede's Saturday soup kitchen and at a few others nearby throughout the week—saves on food costs."

"Good idea. But really sorry that you are going through this."

"Thank you. They leave me alone there, don't pry into my life. I did ask to speak to one of the priests a couple times, I felt so troubled, and he was good to me, listened to me. But unless I make a move to talk, people there tend to treat me pretty much like I'm invisible, which doesn't really bother me. At least it's peaceful. That's why I was surprised when you said hello to me after the service today."

"God's frozen people?" I quipped, remembering a phrase my mother had used from time to time about Episcopalians and their very polite, rather aloof ways.

"Ha! Yes."

Our food was served, we took long sips of beer, and I was eager to see whether Craig would share with me that he'd been called in for questioning by the police in connection with Claire's and Frances's cases.

"The police took me in for questioning a few days ago," he murmured very quietly.

I feigned surprise. "What? Took you in? For what?"

"Someone recalled seeing me on the church grounds in the evening the week of the…assaults. Must have been one of the priests, who live on site in that little square on the south side of the church."

"I've seen that square," I said simply.

"It's true, I *was* on the grounds that week."

I looked up from my greasy tacos directly into Craig's eyes, feeling for the first time a little uneasy in his company. I swallowed hard and felt a sliver of poorly chewed tortilla shell scrape down my throat. "For…what reason?" I asked gently, reaching for my beer.

"I'm ashamed to admit it, but for food. These good priests, all clad in their clerical black each day, and in their shiny vestments on Sunday, hold pretty lavish events many evenings, wining and dining their donors, I guess. I'd seen catering trucks delivering beautiful trays of food—shrimp, ham, assorted raw vegetables, pastries, you know—on several occasions, early evening, and I started to wonder whether they might also throw quite a bit out after these events. So one night around 8:45 I quietly checked around the back of the rectory, where Father Bakewell lives, and a domestic servant was taking out empty wine bottles and various sacks. So I went up to him and said, 'Hey man, if you are throwing any food out, I could really use some help.' This worker, an older black guy, was very nice to me. 'Sure,' he said, 'I'll bring you some.' So I began to look out for those catering and delivery trucks, and later on those evenings I would go back behind the rectory, tap very quietly at the back service door, and this Christian servant would slip me small bags full of vegetables, cheese, sometimes ham and desserts. Cedric, good man."

"Wow." I didn't know what else to say.

"Wow indeed. It's amazing what we are driven to do when times get hard, no? But maybe you've never been there."

"Several of my ancestors were known to have fled Ireland in the 1800s during the famine years.

You know, when the potato crops failed year after year and England was of no help. A lot of wretched stories about hunger and starvation came down to us in our family. I think I understand," I said.

"Wow. Really. That's impressive."

"Suffering abounds."

"So you see, after that one woman was found dead—"

"Claire."

"Claire, okay, and then your sister collapsed, someone at Saint Bede's got the idea that I might have had something to do with all that. So the police hauled me in for questioning. I told them everything I just told you, and I was able to call Father Blum and ask him to come vouch for me, and well, they kept me one more night, apparently did more checking, and then let me go, convinced that I had nothing to do with those cases, thank God, which I *didn't,* let me assure you, Phoebe."

"I believe you, Craig," I said, and we each took deep breaths and reached for our beers. "You said back in the church that hair-raising things happened there…"

"Yes, I did."

"What did you mean?"

"Well, one was just the lives of luxury that these priests live behind the scenes, the fancy food and parties. Have you noticed that most of them are overweight? No surprise. Poor servants of Christ and all. But more than that. When I was collecting food for a couple weeks at the rectory, it was easy on calm nights to hear scattered bits of conversation coming from within, not just there, but as I left, near the other staff apartments. It's a very quiet square, you know, well set back from the street. One night I heard an argument, two loud voices wafting down from the apartments area."

"Not the rectory itself?"

"No, over on the side, where I guess other clergy and some music staff live."

"Could you hear the exact words?"

"At times, but not always. But at various points I heard quite a bit. One said, 'You have the most *antiquated views imaginable!* This is not the *sixteenth century*—you do realize that?' The other shot back, 'With only *your* choices in music, this place would go to *hell in a hand basket!* Contemporary *rubbish!*'"

I grinned slightly. The culture wars. "Well, disagreement over service music doesn't sound too horrible or unexpected. Was one of the men speaking the music director, Averill Page?"

"Maybe, not sure," said Craig. "But get this. I paused for a moment, enjoying the wrangling between these not-so-decorous church personages, and then one said, 'Just be careful with the boy. He's so young—and you're *not.* And your expressions are not as veiled as you think!'"

"The *boy*? Meaning?"

"No idea. An acolyte? Or one of the singers? God forbid one of the kid choristers!

They didn't name him. It was already late and I knew I shouldn't linger, so I moved on, off the grounds, and back to my room. But you can imagine what I was thinking. *God! Clergy and boys. When will that ever end?*"

"Saint Bede's is an Episcopal Church, not a Roman Catholic one," I remarked. "Priests can get married there."

"I realize that. But gays are also very welcome there—basically a fine thing—unlike in the Roman institution. I sit observing the choir most Sundays, see them processing in and out, winking across at each other in those chancel choir stalls when the sermon goes on a bit too long and they think no one is paying attention to them. I start to see the flirtations among them all."

"Oh, fascinating!" I said, wondering whether we were now getting on to matters that might in the end shed some light on Claire's and my sister's fates. "So…?"

"So I think one or more of these churchmen is up to no good. I mean, it didn't sound as if a mutual relationship was being discussed. Rather some sort of pursuit or conquest… I don't know, but I didn't like the sound of it."

"Wow," I murmured, then fell into silence to ponder a moment. What could this have to do with Claire and Frances?

"But what about the women singers?" I asked.

"Oh, you can perceive the vying among the men for their attention, too. In fact, I saw one of the singers on one side of the chancel—"

I interjected, "I think there are two singing groups, one pro and one amateur, and they sit on opposite sides."

"Okay," said Craig. "Whatever. This guy was tall, blond, with a chic sort of haircut. He was smiling away over at one of the women singers on the other side, and she was obviously tickled to death at the attention. Amazing what you can notice if you really focus in."

I rapidly clicked through memories of Frances's emails and wondered whether this was the tenor Frances had met on the subway platform named Vincent.

"I guess it's natural that singers would flirt with each other."

"Sure. But then a couple weeks later, I noticed that this blond Romeo was looking over at that same woman with a sort of scorn in his eyes, and she was not meeting his gaze."

"You could really see that?"

"When I was a high-school teacher, I had to be very attuned to student behavior. I got good at figuring out what was going on by observing carefully at a certain distance."

"Okay, that makes sense. So maybe the romance between those two had soured?"

"Seemed like it."

"Which woman was it?"

"There are two singers on that side who resemble each other, both pretty and with long shiny black hair. It was one of them."

"Oh! My sister Frances has long dark hair. And Claire, too. *Had,* I should say," and Craig and I looked down silently into our now empty plates.

I rallied. "This is interesting, Craig. This might be helpful. I'd been wondering whether any kind of romantic rivalry was going on among the singers. After all, both the women who were attacked—I'm assuming they were attacked—that night were singers—singers similar in appearance, in fact! And there had been chorus rehearsal that night."

"Anything's possible," said Craig, crumpling his paper napkin into a tight ball and dropping it onto his plate.

I nodded and said a little tiredly, "A huge muddle still. And the police are clearly moving only at a snail's pace. But I'm going to root around a bit… Not sure how, but I'm determined to get to the bottom of all this."

"Don't blame you in the least."

"Craig, I'm sorry, but just one more thing," and I inhaled silently and deeply, girding myself. "I hate to ask you this, but were you actually on the grounds the night of April 22, that wretched Thursday evening?"

"Yes, I was. I'd seen *ye olde* catering truck around 6 p.m. and so returned around 8:45 for the usual. But I didn't stay long since I could hear the singers over at the hall and knew they'd be finishing their rehearsal soon. Cedric gave me a nice leftovers bag and I skedaddled. As I told you, when the police called me in, I admitted to them everything about my food collection, and—I forgot to mention this!—Cedric was also summoned down to the station. He vouched for me, along with Father Blum, as I told you. Thank God for both those guys."

"Right, I see. Yes, very fortunate. I believe you, Craig," I assured him, and I did, looking fully into the bluer-than-blue eyes of this poor thin former mathematics teacher. "And I thank you sincerely for this conversation." I signaled for the waiter, and I paid the bill for both of us.

Out on the street once more, I said softly to Craig, "I'm off back now to the hospital. Every day we hope that Frances will wake up. Obviously, when she does, there's a good chance we'll learn a lot more about what happened that night."

He responded in an equally quiet tone, shaking his head. "Terrible, whatever happened, and as I say, it's certainly not heaven on earth there at lovely Saint Bede's."

"Seems churches turn out to have just as many warped characters as most of the other organizations human beings have created over the millennia, no?"

"You're absolutely right about that! I mean, the light and the dark exist side by side, *everywhere.*"

7 ✠ May 11

A stroke of luck today in running into Father Radcliffe Sauer as I was on my way to the precinct to try to speak with Detective Morales.

"Oh, excuse me," I said, crossing paths with a black-clad white-collared figure with black-framed glasses walking with measured pace along the avenue. "Aren't you Father Sauer?"

The short, slightly rotund figure stopped and looked at me with piercing gaze, then smiled and said, "Indeed I am."

"Forgive me, but I am Phoebe Overbridge, Frances's sister—do you remember me? I have been to your services a couple of times. I'm here in town as you may know…"

"Yes, Phoebe, I know, I remember," he said quickly. "We met briefly about a week ago. I am terribly, terribly sorry about everything that has happened. We are at a loss. How is Frances?"

"She is still unconscious. The doctor tells me she has moments when she comes out of it, but these are brief flashes. He is optimistic that she will recover, but the longer this goes on"—and here I shook my head sadly and looked at my feet—"you can understand."

Father Sauer nodded and silently presented a genuinely mournful countenance, and we both sighed deeply.

"Well," I continued, "I was just on my way to try to talk with Detective Morales. Do you know whether anything further has come to light?"

Father Sauer glanced away briefly, rubbed his chin, and then said, "Not to my knowledge. I believe they took someone in for questioning but released him, no evidence to hold him."

I thought, of course, of Craig Scranch but said nothing. "Father Sauer, would you have perhaps fifteen minutes to talk with me? I am desperate for some answers here."

"I'm sure I will have nothing that could be of any help, but certainly. Someone just canceled an appointment and I was going to the café for a coffee. Would you like to join me? Or perhaps in fact it would be better to speak more privately."

We ended up with two take-out cappuccinos, sitting on a park bench under a leafy plane tree, and since it was just 10:30 in the morning, only a few joggers and women with baby strollers were about, passing to and fro in front of us.

I began, "Frances has written me many emails describing how much she loves singing in the chorus at Saint Bede's."

"So nice to hear that! The chorus makes a valuable contribution to our worship. Of course, the pro choir are the most highly musically trained, but curiously, we see that it is chorus members who take communion, most of them, and very few of the choir. Some of the older chorus members also make very generous contributions to the church, for which we are truly grateful."

I nodded and said, "I suppose for the choir, singing is their job and they may or may not be religiously inclined."

"True. But all singers recognize the richness of the sacred music repertoire, and there are many excellent church jobs for trained singers all over town. Most large city churches in fact now have a core of professional singers as well as a community chorus—as we do at Saint Bede's—that participates regularly in the services. We also have a children's choir, as you may know."

"Boys *and* girls, I believe?"

"Yes," said Father Sauer crisply. "Of course, the Anglican traditional boys' choirs go back centuries, and one would have to say that their sound is the most pure and lofty, if you will permit me. But naturally in this day and age, one cannot reasonably exclude girls."

"I would hope not," I rejoined quickly. "Reason is a good thing…"

"I did not mean to imply otherwise, my dear," said Father Sauer smiling. "I confess to being a traditionalist in temperament: I cherish the old ways—the greater emphasis on solemnity, dignity, decorum. But our Anglican/Episcopal Church is firmly built on three solid foundations: scripture, tradition, and reason. Without all three elements, it becomes unbalanced. Too much scripture and you get the raving fundamentalists. Too much tradition and you get the sclerotic Romans. Too much reason and you get…"

"Atheists?" I suggested.

He gave me a slightly sharp look and then said, "The scoffers. The materialists. The New-Agers. And yes, sometimes the atheists. Although the atheists, mind you, sometimes get pretty unreasonable and fanatical in their rejection of religion. Their minds cease to be open. Which is not really reasonable, I think you would agree?"

"You have a point."

"Reason ideally means common sense, respect for the spirit *and* for the flesh we all happen to be living in, in this world. It also means listening, weighing evidence, analyzing, and refraining from judgment whenever possible, since only God knows the entire story and especially the true motivations behind human actions. The Romans, you know, find us wishy-washy, but we find them overly prone to condemn."

I was becoming more and more impressed with Father Sauer's views. As he paused for a brief sip of coffee, I thought to myself that prior to this conversation I had imagined him to be otherwise, a sort of dull, dry academic, and I felt a bit ashamed of myself.

"So in the Episcopal Church," he sailed on, "we have a *duty* to maintain all three foundations of the church, and, going back to the subject of music, given the generally excessively liberal tenor of these times, this is why I personally am in favor of featuring the very best of our ancient musical tradition."

"To counterbalance the more modern stuff?"

"Yes, the *jazz anthems,* as I call them." He grimaced with good nature. "I realize that we must adjust with the times and that different music appeals to different people, but I do fear that the love of the classics is waning from *lack of exposure,* and this is why I'm always pressing at Saint Bede's for inclusion of composers like Byrd, Tallis, Palestrina, Bach, of course, Handel…"

"Absolutely," I responded. "I think Frances is also rather a traditionalist in her tastes."

Our gaze was suddenly directed to a wiry male jogger wearing a rainbow-patterned t-shirt, yellow shorts, and a pink hairband around his sweaty forehead, his long wavy hair flying behind him as he dashed past. He was followed by a young woman in a black cap and long black skirt and tights jogging slowly, and then by an older woman in a shiny blue Lycra top and shorts pushing a sturdy baby carriage at quite a fast trot.

"Yes," said Father Sauer with a smile. "We are blessed with great diversity here in this amazing city. It is never dull."

"I see why Frances wanted to move here," I remarked (rather untruthfully, I confess). "You would have to say that we are much less interesting in the small California town we were raised in, where my husband and I still live now. But we have better weather, and less crime."

"I love California!" responded Father Sauer. "Last year I spent three months in residence as a guest priest and lecturer in a small southern California parish on the coast. Never felt so healthy in my life!"

"All that sunshine, the vitamin D, the sea air…"

"Yes."

"As for crime, sorry to bring the conversation back to this, but how on earth are we going to get to the bottom of what happened to Claire and Frances? Are there any weird dynamics at play at Saint Bede's that you think could have anything to do with these assaults?"

Father Sauer swiveled to face me more directly and said, "I have not spoken about this with anyone, but Phoebe, I do believe there may be something."

With raised eyebrows and parted lips, I waited silently for him to go on.

"Vincent Flaxtin. You know the good-looking blond tenor. During various services, I would see him looking across to Claire—you know the choir and the chorus sit on opposite sides of the chancel. I think he was quite in love with her. But apparently Victor Boindon, one of the basses, also became interested in her. I happened to run into Claire and Vincent in the French café once—across from the church, where we got our cappuccinos just now, in fact—and, well, it's none of my business, but they looked pretty dewy-eyed sitting gazing at each other over their cherry tarts, and I thought, Ah, another happy couple brought together by the church! But then a week or so later, I saw Claire there with *Victor,* and at church I saw distinctly morose and bitter glances going from Vincent over to Claire, who refused to meet his eyes."

"Oh, dear, I see. A bad break-up, a harsh rejection."

"Apparently. Vincent has been with us for about three years, a dashing figure and excellent tenor, but also, we've noticed, quite outspoken at times, a bit critical, gets temperamental, angry."

"Really?"

"Once, he came to me in my office and pronounced, 'Father Sauer, as much as I enjoy singing at Saint Bede's, the clouds of incense used during the services each week really are *insufferable!'* I was taken aback. The use of fragrant incense, as you may know, goes back centuries and centuries in the Christian Church, a symbol of the prayers of the faithful rising to heaven."

I recalled silently that Frances had complained once in an email of said incense. "What exactly was Vincent's objection?" I asked.

"He said he had asthma and found the incense aggravating. He complained of having to take extra medication before singing in the services: 'I'm fed up with having to use an inhaler so often!' as I recall. He remarked that Caroline, the choristers' chaperone, had once mentioned to him that one of the girl singers also suffered from asthma and detested the incense—her mother had called to complain, and so forth. Vincent then got on his high horse and cited Isaiah, you know that line: 'Bring no more vain oblations; incense is an abomination unto me.' He got quite worked up, banged the top of my desk! However, these practices have to be understood *in context*..."

"Hmm," I murmured. "Yet understandable. My husband is allergic to cats, really miserable if he unexpectedly finds himself in some social situation at one of our friends' homes where cat hair is everywhere on the furniture..."

"Yes, yes, I realize. Allergies can be very unpleasant."

"And can be dangerous."

"Well," said Father Sauer, and then paused to eye a trim fellow priest all in black with crisp white collar striding past. "People do have to consider these things when deciding to sing at Saint Bede's. We are reluctant to discontinue the use of incense—"

"Tradition?" I suggested, remembering the three foundations.

Father Sauer's eyes narrowed once more as he met my gaze, but he said evenly, "Yes, a beautiful tradition. But we are actually in the process of discussing how we might modify the use of incense—we are not insensitive, after all. But my point is that during this interchange, I observed how upset Vincent was, and how angrily he expressed himself. It seemed a bit over the top, actually."

"So you are saying…?"

"Merely that he is quite temperamental, it appears. If Claire rejected him, he might have reacted badly."

"Oh!" I cried, looking fully into Father Sauer's eyes, steely behind his thick black-framed glasses. "You mean, you think he could be capable of violence?"

"It is possible," he replied. "I do believe that is possible."

8 ✠ May 12

This morning I realized that Averill Page would be back in town by now from his Germany trip, but of course only just, and what real right did I have to ask to talk with him? Or with Vincent? I decided I would plan to go to church yet again on Sunday and in the meantime today try to talk with Detective Morales. After checking in at the hospital room and finding Frances unchanged, I wiped away tears and headed up the block and east, reflecting on the various conversations I'd had so far with people associated with Saint Bede's. They all seem very decent people, in fact, but it occurs to me: can I really believe everything any one of them has told me? And what have they chosen *not* to tell me?

I reached the precinct and they told me Detective Morales would be back in about thirty minutes, so I sat down to wait on a hard wooden bench. When he strode in, snappily attired in tight black jeans, black leather jacket, and sleek brown brogues, I stood and extended my hand. "Phoebe Overbridge," I reminded him, "Frances Whitestone's sister."

"Mrs. Overbridge," he said, shaking my hand.

"If you could spare five minutes..."

"Of course," he replied, and we walked a short distance down a drab hallway to his cluttered office, where we entered but remained standing.

"Has anything become clear yet?"

"We have questioned every single staff person at Saint Bede's one by one, and we also questioned a neighborhood man, but so far, I'm sorry to say, no real progress."

I wondered silently whether he knew about Claire's romantic entanglements, or about what might be brewing behind that disturbing "Be careful with the boy!" overheard by Craig Scranch, which I assumed Craig had shared with him. So to begin, I cautiously remarked, "I have attended Sunday services there twice now, and I did briefly talk with a couple of the clergy and one singer. There are tensions there between various people..."

"There always are," interjected Pandolfo Morales. "At churches, at offices, at factories—that goes without saying."

"Of course." I felt slightly rebuffed.

"We need to find *evidence,* which is sorely lacking here so far. I know how frustrated you must be, Mrs. Overbridge, but I can't discuss the details of the investigation, as you must understand. But we are on it every day, and I will let you know anything relevant as soon as I can."

"I'll appreciate that," I said softly, feeling chastened. "You know I'm staying at Frances's apartment, and you have my cell number."

"Yes. Thank you." At that moment his desk phone rang. He said, "Excuse me," and I turned to hurry out of the precinct offices, feeling very much that I needed to stay *on it* myself, every single day, too, or this could drag on for months.

So after grabbing lunch at a small pizzeria, I returned to Saint Bede's, with the plan of trying to talk with the church secretary Everild. Alas, she was out today. And now it's raining, and I'm back at Frances's silent bedside. I'm going to scroll back even further in her emails…

*

September 24

Dear Phoebe,

Well, it is Thursday and you know I should be gearing up for chorus rehearsal tonight! It's a wonderfully warm afternoon, perfect for going out for an early dinner at some outdoor café with a wee tipple of lovely red wine, and then going on to rehearsal. But no. Despite a marvelous rebirth of my singing self with this wonderful group in late August, something unexpected happened last week. Our first two Sundays had featured Stanford, Parry, Mozart, with organ preludes and postludes by Bach and Widor, and I was over the moon, thoroughly delighted! Then last Thursday, Doug and Caspar introduced the work we would be singing for the big Saint Francis Day service, apparently always the first Sunday in October. Well, Saint Francis is near and dear to my heart in so many ways, but especially for his rejection of all the pomp and material richness of the church, and for his kindness to animals! They passed out a sturdily bound score with a photograph of a lush cascading waterfall on the cover, and we began to read through it. A sort of jazz mass! With animal and nature sounds accompanying and sometimes displacing regular melodies and harmonies, which I found very difficult to sight-read. I confess, Phoebe, I felt totally out of my depth and comfort zone. Many of the chorus members seemed to know the work, so fortunately I was able to follow along and not stick out like a sore thumb. We worked the entire rehearsal on this New Creation Mass, *as it is called (by a composer I've never heard of), and frankly it made my skin crawl! I had not realized that Saint Bede's went in for this sort of music.*

Well, in any case, I kept a good face on, as best I could anyway. When this rehearsal finally ended at 9:00, I walked out with a group of sopranos and altos and fell into step with one of the altos, Claire, a pretty woman a bit younger than I, from Montreal. We chatted about the weather a moment, and then, once we were clear of other chorus members, she muttered, "I can't stand that piece."

"The New Creation Mass?*"*

"Yes. Not my thing at all. Feels more like chaos than creation, quelle horreur! *I can't stand really new-age stuff! And they do it every year, year after year, for Saint Francis Day."*

"I've never sung anything like it before, and I can't say I really enjoyed that read-through."

"It's the only really 'way-out' work Saint Bede's features each year, at least involving us, the chorus—otherwise I might seriously reconsider my decision to sing

there! It's part of a huge spectacle they create for Saint Francis Day, which bothers me even more than the music: they bring in very large and exotic animals to the service."

"Oh! Why?"

"A 'blessing of the animals' tradition. Many churches observe this on Saint Francis Day, but most simply have the congregation, those who want to, bring their pets in for a blessing—dogs and cats, the odd hamster—sometimes a few social deviants bring in their pet snakes. But at big Saint Bede's, maybe because they have the space, they truck in llamas and horses…"

I gasped in amazement.

"…yes, and they even brought in an elephant one year!"

"But why, on earth?"

"Le fric. *To make money."*

I laughed.

"You remember what Juvenal, the Roman poet, wrote, 'Bread and circuses.' That's what people want. That's what they clamor for. I'm not sure how the tradition started, but the clergy soon realized that people in the neighborhood who usually did not bother coming to church were fascinated by the Saint Francis Day animal parade. Year after year more and more people began to attend this service as larger and larger animals were featured, and it became a trendy New York thing to do, a 'Wow!' sort of event. And Saint Bede's is very large, as you know. Each year now on that sacred feast of the humble friar named Francis, this place is packed to the rafters with local people, musicians, dancers, and animals small and large—all producing an unbearable cacophony!

Can you imagine how Francis himself would have reacted to this? Bref, *more people in the pews means more money tossed into the collection plates when they are passed around. Saint Bede's brings in thousands of dollars every Saint Francis Day."*

"Wow. Like a hit Broadway show."

"C'est exact," *said Claire. "But do you think the animals like it?* Mon Dieu, *it pains me. They truck the large animals in from zoos and animal refuges and whatnot, but of course no animal wants to be forced into a truck or onto those stone-cold floors, surrounded by hundreds of other unfamiliar animals. And that atrocity we sing, that* New Creation Mass *with its various animal and earth sounds and the piercing saxophone line, just sets all the animals off. You see hoofs stomping, the horse shaking its head, dogs howling and barking, cats shrieking—it's a nightmare, a madhouse."*

"But how can they keep doing this?"

"Well might you ask! I suppose they think they are presenting to the city a grand symbol of nature in harmony, respect and love for all the animals, the ocean, the forests, blah blah blah. So ironic, with all that ear-splitting noise and discomfort! But it's just all for the money. The only times the animals are fairly quiet and still are during the very quietest parts of the service, but these interludes don't last long. It's a horrible circus, plain and simple." Claire paused and we glanced briefly directly into each other's eyes.

I felt appalled and worried by everything she was so painfully describing. I said, "I'm not sure I'm going to be able to handle all this. And I have allergies to cat dander, too, and to other things."

"This is my third year with the chorus, but you know, I decided during rehearsal tonight that I am going to boycott this particular service now. I can't stand the music or the whole animal exploitation spectacle. And in fact I am finally going to write to the music directors and clergy about this."

"It's useful to hear you say all this," I confessed. "I know I would be terribly uncomfortable during that service, too, and I agree that the piece is, well, certainly not my thing either. It's very hard to sing works you don't like."

"I did it for two years, but now, no, too hard, too painful! Why should I go through that yet again this year? J'en ai assez. *And think about it: all over the world cities are banning circuses as inhumane. It's wrong to use poor dear animals for the entertainment of ignorant human beings. Saint Bede's is really behind the times, shamefully."*

"I agree with you, Claire!" I cried. "I really do. I adore animals, and alongside circuses I also hate zoos and aquariums and all those sorts of creature prisons. Animals should live freely."

"What would *Saint Francis say!"*

We'd reached a corner market, where Claire indicated she was going to pick up some groceries before heading home. We stopped and faced each other. "You know, Claire," I said, "I'm really glad you told me about all this. I'm new at the church and I don't want to rock the boat at this point, but I'm going to skip this service, too, I've decided. I'll just inform the music directors that I see I have a calendar conflict on that day that cannot be avoided, very sorry."

So, Phoebe, this is why, here on this lovely September Thursday afternoon, I am not *preparing for chorus rehearsal. I feel a bit guilty, but I did email the directors a couple days after the conversation with Claire, and they were fine with it. I figure things might change by next year—I hope I don't have to make excuses every fall as Saint Francis Day rolls around. Anyway, that's far in the future. I am basically so happy to be back in a choir, and I don't want to make waves. If this chorus is like others I was in years ago, singers probably* all *at various points take weeks off—we are just volunteers, after all, not paid singers. The paid choir holds everything down Sunday after Sunday.*

Will sign off for now, dear Sis, thinking of you all out there in old California, hoping the orchards are as bounteous as ever and that you are wearing sunscreen—please don't forget!

Love, Frances

9 ✠ May 13

A very full day! Not only did I manage to find Everild in her office, but I found myself in the role of undercover sleuth later in the day at the Café Lyonnais across from the church. But everything in order.

First, another agonizing sit next to Frances from 9:00 until 10:00 this morning—I've taken to chattering to her softly as I sit, in a calm, non-stop way, about things from our childhood, orchard updates from Matt, anything that is pleasant and familiar, hoping that the sound of my voice will penetrate one of these days and that she will rise out of her coma. Dr. Benedetto Lasso said today that one of the aides, as she was taking Frances's blood pressure around 6:30, heard her mumble something! "Oh!" I cried. "What did she say?" Indecipherable. She was shaking her head a bit from side to side as if denying something, the aide said, and mumbled, *"Nomnah, nomnahtasneh"*—something to that effect.

"What on earth?" I said.

"No-I'm-not? No I'm not…something," suggested Dr. Lasso.

"Asneh? Meaning?"

"No idea. But this is a good sign. She may well be coming round." And Dr. Lasso described that he was going to change her nutrition slightly and increase the television-on time from three to five hours throughout the day, along with moving her bed closer to the window in the hopes that the changes in natural light from dawn to dusk might stimulate her. I thought these were good ideas.

"May I bring a radio in?" I asked. "Frances is a choir singer, as you know, and loves classical music. That might work wonders." I felt stupid not to have thought of this sooner.

"Absolutely fine," responded the doctor.

*

Now as for Everild, I arrived at Saint Bede's at about 10:30, went straight to the rectory, and was about to knock when the rector opened the heavy carved wooden door and stepped out.

"Father Bakewell," I said. "Hello. Good morning."

"Good morning, Phoebe," he said with a cloud across his brow. He held a folder and a Bible in his hands and looked to be on his way to some appointment.

"Sorry to disturb you," I began.

"No disturbance. I was just going across to meet with Father Sauer about a few points of liturgy for Sunday. May I help you? And how is Frances?"

"She is about the same, but an aide heard her apparently mumble a few words early this morning. The doctor thinks she may be slowly, slowly coming round."

Without changing his somber and preoccupied expression, Father Bakewell said, "Good. *Very* good, my dear. We can only hope and pray, hope and pray."

"I was wondering whether I might talk just briefly with Everild, the church secretary? Frances mentioned her once in an email—I think Frances has donated a bit of money to the church and had some contact once with Everild…"

"Certainly. She is in right now. Just follow that little hallway to the left, and her office is the first door you come to also on the left."

I thanked him and he dashed off.

I knocked softly at the open door and a lean older woman with stylish wavy grey hair dressed in a pale-blue linen suit looked up at me. Her very sharp brown eyes focused on me from behind red plastic round-framed glasses. "Yes?" she asked.

"Everild Dunne? Very sorry to disturb you, but I am Mrs. Phoebe Overbridge, Frances Whitestone's older sister, and I wondered whether you could spare just fifteen minutes or so to talk with me?"

"Oh, my goodness. Please come in. Of course." She sprang up with unexpected agility and came round from behind her desk to extend her hand, which I took and squeezed gently. "Please sit down," she said, drawing up a small upholstered armchair to the side of her desk. "Would you like some tea?" she asked.

"No, I'm fine, but thank you."

Everild returned to her swivel chair behind her desk and sat down. I noticed that her desk was very neat, with a laptop, several stacks of papers, and a large vase full of fragrant pink roses. Seeing me glance admiringly at the flowers, she said, "From my daughter in California. It was my birthday two days ago."

"Oh, your daughter lives in California? My husband and I live there, too, and Frances and I grew up there. Mid-coast area. Frances has only been in New York for less than a year."

Everild smiled and said, "Yes, my Erlina lives in West Los Angeles. She's a teacher, married a fellow graduate student years ago who craved the ocean, palm trees, and year-round heat and was determined to leave New York winters far behind."

"We're in Santa Maria, just outside, really. We run a juice business with our own orchards. Orange and lemon, as you might imagine."

"Lovely."

A pause ensued, Everild looked at me with a warm yet penetrating gaze, and I realized that she must be quite busy and that I should cut to the chase. I suddenly felt a bit nervous.

"I'm trying to figure out…trying to discover what happened that night when Frances was injured. As you can imagine," I said, then realized with some embarrassment that I'd used pretty much the same phrase just a moment ago. *Get a grip, Phoebe, get a grip.*

"Of course."

"Frances is a good singer, a soprano, absolutely loves classical music, was thrilled to move to New York, which has always fascinated her. She found a good job in an artsy non-profit organization. And she's a very sweet person," I added, and then unexpectedly found myself unable to speak, nearly strangled with emotion.

Showing compassion and concern, Everild immediately responded, "Poor, poor thing. We are so devastated by what happened here a few weeks ago. You can't imagine the state we are all in, even though everyone tries not to show it, tries just to soldier on bravely. I am terribly sorry, my dear."

I thanked her and brushed away a few tears. I continued. "Did you—do you know Frances at all?"

"No, I don't, I'm sorry to say. She has generously contributed some money to Saint Bede's, and I process these donations. I had an assistant helping with that, actually, for a short time, but he turned out to be a sad disappointment. Such is life. So I have personally deposited Frances's checks in our church account over at the bank. It's terribly kind of her, I must say."

"She's been very happy here—or was, up until that night."

Everild went on. "I also attend Sunday services, and so of course I see all of the singers up there most every week. I've worked here now for donkey's years, and I get to know most of the singers, since sooner or later most will have some business with the church office. But Frances of course is quite new, and I don't think she's ever actually stopped by the office."

I pondered this. Then I decided to divulge a bit more information to Everild than I had done in previous conversations with Saint Bede's staff. "Everild, I'll be frank with you. Over the past two weeks I've had a few conversations with people here at the church—I have also been attending on Sunday mornings. Apparently a couple of the men were interested in Claire—not surprising, of course, I hear she was quite pretty—"

"Yes, that long glossy black hair and a serene, Madonna sort of face. A kindergarten teacher. Such a tragedy."

"Yes. Well, someone in the congregation mentioned that he thought the tall blond tenor liked her. I believe his name is Vincent."

"Yes, Vincent Flaxtin," replied Everild with a slight sharpening around the corners of her eyes.

"I also heard that he was a rather temperamental sort of character, had made some complaints…"

"He complained about our use of incense, a long tradition here. I happened to overhear part of that conversation, I believe with Father Sauer, one day. Yes, Vincent was vexed and got a bit hot under the collar. Incense certainly can be aggravating to some people, I do realize."

"Yes, understandable. He apparently was involved with Claire, or beginning to date her, but then was rejected? I'm just trying to assess whether he might be the type to hit or shove a woman in anger."

Everild looked at me with serious eyes a moment, then looked at her keyboard. "Phoebe, this is a sensitive issue, of course, but I completely understand how urgently you want to figure out what happened to your sister, which could very well be connected, somehow, with Claire's tragedy. And I know the police investigation is pretty much stalled at this point. I do want to help you. So I will tell you, confidentially, that yes, I have a bad feeling about Vincent. He's been here for about three years, and his voice is excellent, a truly wonderful tenor. I believe he gets engagements at major venues around town—and in that way we are lucky to have him. But he is a sort of *diva.* I wonder, is that word used for men as well as women? In any case, he does have a hot temper. I was sitting in on a rehearsal one evening for our big Christmas Concert here, which is so beautiful every year, and I recall an incident. Vincent had a solo section, and Averill apparently was rushing him, or not waiting long enough after a *fermata* before Vincent's entrance, and after a couple of false starts, or bungled moments, Vincent burst out in a really testy manner. All heads turned toward him and you could hear a pin drop in there, everyone was so flabbergasted! Vincent then immediately apologized, saying, "Sorry to mimic an erupting volcano," and his tone was so soft and convincing that everyone then burst out laughing. A weird moment. It passed. Musicians, you know. They went on to work out the passage, the timing, but for me, looking on, I have to say that at that moment of anger, Vincent looked like a deranged person. So to answer your question, yes, I think he is the sort of man who would be capable of striking a woman in anger."

"Well!"

"Yes."

"Hmm. Where to go from here?" I pondered aloud.

Everild continued. "I think the bass Victor was also dating Claire. As I recall, Claire and Vincent had had sweet eyes for each other, and then one Sunday all that had clearly ended, and I noticed her walking out after the service with Victor. Maybe you should talk with Victor."

I reflected that I *had* talked with Victor but recalled no mention of Vincent. "Yes," I responded. "Good idea. I will see if I can manage that." *What a wretched soap opera,* I thought to myself. *Why did Frances ever leave Santa Maria for all this high-culture-big-city turmoil?*

"Vincent is quite young, I think?" I asked Everild.

"Not as young as he looks, late-thirties, in fact. But he does have that ever-youthful appearance, fresh rosy face and full head of blond hair. He'll probably look much younger than his actual age for many years to come. Like a boy!"

"I was thinking of that. Is there any chance Vincent could be…gay? Or bisexual?"

"Of course," said Everild with unexpected promptness and calm. "Here in the Episcopal Church, everyone is welcome, and nothing is surprising. We are considered probably the most liberal and open denomination of them all. We tend to have many gay and lesbian congregants, singers, even clergy. Bisexual—I'm not really up to speed on that, but no doubt. Vincent could very well be bisexual."

"Clergy? Are any of the clergy gay or bisexual?"

Everild looked down for a moment and squeezed the fingers of one hand vigorously. "For several years, yes, one of our junior priests was a gay man, very nice, gentle person. Very reserved, quiet. Never heard a complaint about him. He left to move to San Francisco, I believe."

Thinking of the ominous-sounding utterance that Craig had overheard in the square, "Just be careful with the boy!" I nervously considered how to phrase my next question. "I'll tell you something, Everild," I began, deciding to be plain. "A person I talked with recently from the congregation confided that he had overheard something rather pointed and worrisome, and he seems to be pretty sure that one of the staff, either clergy or music staff, is pursuing a boy here. He actually heard the word *boy* used, but I have no idea whom he meant. Acolyte? Chorister? Young singer? Could the boy be Vincent, or even Caspar? Could there have been—or is there—competition for Vincent or Caspar from women and men alike? I'm sorry to ask such probing questions, but do you have any idea whom he may have been referring to?"

Everild's eyebrows rose just slightly and she looked away to the wall, where her eyes rested on a thickly painted canvas, rather cubist-expressionist in style, in dark blues and purples, of a Madonna and Child. She looked back at me and said with unease, "Very difficult. I'll be quite honest with you, Phoebe. Both Averill Page, the music director, and Father Sauer, our liturgist, are gay, but as for pursuing boys…goodness, I have no idea, really."

I had not realized that Father Sauer was gay! Neither Father Blum nor Father Bakewell had revealed this in our duologues. Victor perhaps was unaware of it. I tried not to let my face show my surprise. I just nodded and hoped Everild would say more.

After a pause, the longtime church secretary, looking uncomfortable, went on. "Averill, you may have observed, is very warm, very *huggy*. When he first came to us as music director here, he had a partner, a man younger than himself, very boyish, I think a clarinetist. To each their own, obviously. But that ended—nothing is entirely private around here, you must know, and tongues are always wagging. Shortly after this, Averill took up with a singer, also younger than himself, and that relationship seemed to last about two years. Then *that* fizzled. For about a year, he seemed to be on his own, but he bought several birds as company."

"Birds?"

"Parakeets, canaries, in cages. He still has quite a few, and he keeps them all in separate cages. He likes to collect 'designer cages,' apparently. He likes the sound of the tweeting, finds it soothing. He sings back to them. I've been to his apartment only twice, and personally, well, I think birds don't belong in cages."

"I agree. Strange. People are so unique, aren't they! Each with their own quirks."

"Yes, completely. Well, then after a while Averill found someone new, a percussionist in the symphony, near to his age, it appears."

Everild and I looked at each other with resigned smiles, each seeming to say, *Well, it is what it is.*

"Averill is in his fifties, then?"

"About fifty-five, I think."

"So…how long has he been with the percussionist?"

"At least three years, I think. Maybe he's settled down. But…"

I waited for Everild to go on.

"I've noticed—and again, you really must keep this to yourself—that Averill is very fond of his young student, our assistant choirmaster, Caspar."

"Ah! I have met Caspar, seems a nice young man."

"Very. And quite handsome."

"But is he gay?" I asked, not choosing to reveal that I'd had a long conversation with Caspar two weeks ago and knew that he wasn't.

"No one really knows. He doesn't seem to have a girlfriend, or a boyfriend. He's quite friendly and warm to everyone, and of course he must get a lot of attention from people his own age."

"And from older gay men?"

"You know that world. There's a lot of…commotion among gay men. I know that Averill has Caspar doing a lot for him, even helping out with photography and whatnot when Averill has big events downtown. It's pretty obvious that he adores Caspar."

"I wonder what Caspar feels!"

"He's Averill's student in conducting and musicology—I believe he's Roman Catholic, by the way, Caspar. He may be in a bit of a bind. He may not have expected this sort of close association to have burgeoned with his academic supervisor when he enrolled at Breconford. Averill is brilliant, of course, a top conductor, acclaimed across the whole country, actually. And he's had many, many students over the years.

You know how critical it is to keep a completely professional stance in schools and universities. I know Caspar feels honored to be learning from him. But, in truth, I've noticed that Caspar does look just a bit uncomfortable at times around Averill, and, well, I just hope that nothing..."

Everild paused, and I nodded and remained silent, and we each pondered how to proceed. My mind was feverishly trying to process everything. Could it have been Father Sauer who shouted at Averill that night about "the boy"? Or the reverse? Was Caspar the boy in question? Or could the boy in fact be Vincent?

"When I was a young naïve college student—and you can imagine how long ago that was!" said Everild with a hoot of laughter "—I dated a man I was crazy about, who turned out to be gay, or bisexual maybe, and I still remember to this day one of his classic lines, after we'd broken up: 'Men are polygamous and brutes.'"

I burst out laughing. Everild began laughing, too, and we dissolved into pure mirth for at least a minute.

"Oh my goodness," I said, gasping for air. "This is a true statement!"

"Those were his exact words, *polygamous and brutes*. As if that explained and mitigated everything. He was English, from London."

"So succinct! I suppose he had choice epithets for us women, too?"

"Slave-drivers. Obsessive-compulsive neurotics."

We both burst once more into fits of laughter.

"The gender wars," I gasped.

"It's a wild, wild world out there."

I knew I should leave and let Everild get back to her work, but wanting to stay on-topic for just a bit longer I said, "Both Caspar and Vincent are very dashing young men, boys, if you like. Do you think Averill or Father Sauer may also be drawn to Vincent?" *What a quagmire this is becoming,* I reflected.

"Yes, Vincent attracts many eyes, and yes, I have seen Father Sauer eyeing both Caspar and Vincent during services. It's amazing how much visual interaction you can notice, observing in the pews during services. Yes, anything's possible—and what a stew, I admit. But it's always like that, anywhere, behind the scenes, don't you think?"

"Not on our orchard farm," I replied a little too quickly. "That is, I've never lived in a big city or been much involved with the arts, so this is all rather unfamiliar to me, to be honest."

Everild smiled. "This is *New York,* my dear."

At that moment, a knock came on the door and Father Bakewell appeared, looking very distraught, his arms laden with blankets.

"Everild, one of the altos just fainted during rehearsal! They've called an ambulance, but please go over to the church with these blankets—I've just grabbed these from the rectory. I'm going to go find Father Blum."

"Goodness!" I cried. "Can I help?"

"Phoebe," Father Bakewell observed. "Thank you, no, we'll manage."

As Everild sprang up, I thanked her quickly for the conversation and made a hasty exit. As I walked down the drive toward the avenue, I wondered why exactly the alto had fainted. I reflected that people of all ages had medical conditions, women were particularly burdened with regular fluctuations in their bodies, and unexpected dehydration was common. How curious I now felt, however, about every single thing that occurred at Saint Bede's! I decided to go across to the Café Lyonnais for a coffee, since I knew some of the singers frequented the place, and with a mysterious instinct that I didn't question, as I crossed the street I put on my medium-tint sunglasses and loosened my hair from its usual pony tail.

*

At the café I settled in at a small table in the back with a cappuccino and a chocolate éclair. I also pulled out from my bag my paperback *Grapes of Wrath* and placed it on the table. I began to read, and to eat and sip as slowly as possible. Within ten minutes, three people, whom I recognized from my attendance at services as Saint Bede's professional choir singers, entered, two women and one man—and one of them was Vincent! His glowing good looks and abundant blond hair were unmistakable. I feigned total absorption in my book and *pâtisserie,* and to my amazement, the trio sat at the table right next to mine. I had never personally met any of them and felt fairly sure that none would recognize me as Frances's sister, but I nevertheless made sure to angle away from them, while keeping a sharp ear directed their way.

"*Merciful God.* Unbelievable," uttered a low-pitched female voice.

"We had just finished the Benedictus, and *thump!* She went down right next to me. Poor Lily!" The other female voice had spoken, higher-pitched.

"Was she ill before the rehearsal, Erin?" asked Vincent.

"No, not that I was aware. But she did mention having rushed, left home late because her aunt had kept her on the phone too long. And I noticed she didn't have a water bottle at hand."

"Lily is just that bit *rotund*—" began Vincent, which was followed by a chirp of laughter from one of the women.

"Shame on you, Rowena!" he chastised. "I just mean that if she got dehydrated—and it is a pretty long mass, that Machaut—"

"Just your choice of words, sorry. You know I love Lily. Yes, and he had us standing in that semicircle with no break for too long. I was actually starting to feel a little achy in the feet."

"Me, too," said Erin.

By that point, in my impromptu role as novice sleuth, I had figured out which voice went with which woman.

"Did she hit her head on the ground? Good Lord, I hope not," said Vincent.

"No, I don't think so."

Vincent went on. "They shooed us out pretty quick, but I saw the paramedics arrive. She'll be all right—I hope."

Rowena observed, "My grandfather has collapsed a couple times in recent months from dehydration. They say that older people don't feel their thirst as keenly as younger people."

"Lily is only about forty, Rowena," said Erin with mild rebuke. "She'll be fine."

A pause ensued and from the corner of my eye I saw my neighbors each take a sip of their drinks.

"Have you noticed," asked Vincent, "that our services seem to be getting longer and longer?"

"Yes!" cried both women simultaneously.

"I mean, this is the great Anglican tradition of church music, of course, but remember Holy Week? Maundy Thursday, nearly two hours—"

"Many feet to wash."

"Then two Good Friday services, each of over two hours."

"After the second one," said Rowena, "I limped home and fell into bed without even washing my face."

"Then the Saturday Easter Vigil!" continued Vincent. "I mean, *really!* How many psalms did we sing? And the anthems, and all those hymns…"

"If you've noticed," said Erin, "Holy Week is one of the only times in the whole year that the pews are pretty full, especially, of course, on Easter…"

"Two and a half hours!" emphasized Rowena. "Easter, I mean."

"…so obviously Saint Bede's must take in a lot via the collection plate that week."

"People come for the drama."

"Isn't that a bit cynical, Vincent?"

"Yes, Erin, it is. I am a cynic, as you know."

They all laughed.

"Well, let me clarify. I think that people do come for a little injection of religion, of spirituality. Especially here in the city—so much loneliness. People really do need something larger than themselves to connect with."

"And they enjoy the music," said Rowena.

"Yes, for sure. But since we see that kind of turn-out only during Holy Week, Christmas, and Saint Francis Day—"

"The Big Animal Circus," interrupted Erin, and they all hooted again.

"—my point being that since apart from those big feasts attendance is pretty mediocre the rest of the year, it's clear that most people are not interested in long, long services every Sunday, as we tend to do them. Tedious, boring. Especially when the sermon goes on too long. People like the periodic spectacles, but most the year I think they prefer having Sunday brunch out with their friends!"

"Very wise, I suppose," observed Rowena.

"But thank God for the ones who attend and who contribute fairly often," said Erin. "Otherwise we wouldn't have jobs!"

"You speak truth," said the tenor.

"Maybe a matter of taste, in the end," said Rowena.

"Yes," said Vincent, "except that I do wonder what God thinks of the really long prayers, long sermons, droning on and on. I mean, I think there are scripture passages about all that, aren't there? 'You think you will be heard for your many words'—some such. And another thing! The incense. Holy God, that's one thing that is really getting to me. Abominable! Didn't Isaiah agree? That man knew how to raise some hell!" The women burst out laughing. "I don't know about you ladies, but I happen to have asthma, and before each service—and sometimes right in the middle of one—I have to use my inhaler! And the kids, the choristers. Have you noticed them coughing every time, after the censor guy does his thing? I sincerely question whether incense is actually good or at all necessary."

"I have to agree," said Rowena, "but God forbid you should mention this to the clergy, especially Father Sauer. You know how they love their traditions there!"

Erin said, "Claire—rest her soul—I think she agreed with you, Vincent, on some of these matters."

"Claire," said Vincent softly, with a notable sombering of tone.

Erin continued. "She mentioned to me once that she found the Saint Francis service very unpalatable, and I used to see her using her folder to wave away the incense—I mean she did that in a subtle way, but she did it."

"Yes, I used to notice that, too," said Rowena.

Vincent remained silent.

"Sorry, Vincent," said Erin. "I know you were dating Claire at one point…"

"Yes, I was. She was an amazing person."

"What happened, can we ask? Why did you break up?" asked Rowena softly.

"Victor."

"She…left you for Victor, really?"

"Yep. Victor the hunk. And the drunk—did you know that? How that guy can drink!"

"No!"

"Yes, dear, he can and he does. But he hides it well. But I can smell it on his breath sometimes, rather often in fact just before evensong. And Claire actually had the gall, before she'd even told me of her feelings, to give me the cold shoulder right after evensong one night. I'd wanted to take her to dinner that night, but she brushed me off, said something like, 'Not tonight, Vin, but we need to talk.' That threw me for a loop, I can tell you! And then a few minutes later, I saw her and Victor walk out of the church together."

"Sounds quite devastating," said Erin.

"It was. I was floored. And angry."

"Sorry Vin," said Rowena kindly. "Really sorry."

"I tried to call her later—she wouldn't answer her phone! *Bitch.*"

"But why exactly do you think she left you for Victor? What was the problem?" asked Erin gently.

"Inscrutable are the ways of women. I tried to arrange to talk with her, but she kept avoiding me! Maddening! And then…never mind. I never got the chance." Vincent emitted an anguished sigh.

A long silence ensued and I made sure not to move a muscle, except to quietly turn a page of my novel. The Café Lyonnais was about half-full at that point, the gentle ambient clatter of cups and plates and the myriad conversations serving as effective white noise to the occupants of each table.

Then Erin asked cautiously, "Did you see her at all that day? I think it was a Thursday, right? The day the chorus rehearses? They found her very early Friday morning…"

"Let's drop it," barked Vincent. "I told you, she kept putting me off."

"Right…"

A pause ensued.

"You cannot *possibly* be suggesting—?!"

"Shh!" said Erin. "Of course not, Vin—we know you better than that!"

"I would hope so!"

Rowena began, "I need to go, I—" and erupted in a coughing fit, which abated after about fifteen seconds. "I'm fine, don't worry," she said finally.

"Look," said Vincent with a tremor in his voice. "This neighborhood is better than it used to be, but you wouldn't exactly call it safe…"

"No place in New York City is safe after dark," interjected Rowena.

"Nighttime is a whole different ball game, we all know that, and there are a lot of homeless people who go to Saint Bede's for the soup kitchen, and who knows what their backgrounds are? They get to know the grounds. There are valuable things there…"

Erin said, "Robbery, you mean. Someone could have been prowling around with the intention of stealing something."

"Of course. The hall where they serve the meals is right next to other rooms—the acolyte room, for example, where they store the big gold crucifixes they use in procession."

"Who would want to steal a crucifix?" asked Rowena.

"Just for example, you goose! Smaller things—the silver communion chalices—I don't know. Or even just a garden-variety mugging…or worse."

"Vincent!"

"Claire was attractive, we all know that, and she dressed well and carried one of those chic designer bags. Could it not have been that she was mugged that night? Struck or pushed in the attack, knocked over? Frances, too, by the same guy, as he ran out."

The two women were silent, and then Erin replied, "Yes. Yes, that is certainly possible."

"It's horrible," added Rowena. "The whole thing makes me shiver."

"The police will figure it out," said Vincent.

"They'd better," said Erin.

"And soon," added Rowena. "Three weeks gone by already! To think that whoever did this is still lurking around…"

"Let's not go there," said Erin. "Enough of this. Let's go. Maybe we should stop back at the church and ask about Lily."

The three gathered up their things and left the café. A few minutes later, I did, too.

10 ✠ May 14

Friday again. After the illuminating but exhausting day yesterday, I collapsed into bed early last night and today was up by 8:00. By 9:00 I was back at the hospital with the portable radio I had found in Frances's closet. Perfect. We tuned it to a classical radio station and placed it on her bedside table. At that moment the announcer introduced and launched a lively movement from a Corelli *concerto grosso*, very upbeat. Did I see a slight smile bloom on Frances's face? Maybe just wishful thinking on my part. No, I don't think she reacted, but this idea is definitely worth trying, as is having the television on for more hours each day. I made sure to let the nurses and Dr. Lasso know to keep the channel on Public Television, as many travel shows and historical British dramas as possible—no sensationalist news or vapid soap operas, please!—and to keep the volume fairly low. They understood and agreed.

Then I left to return to Saint Bede's, feeling very frustrated at the lack of progress in the two cases. As I walked, my brain stewed. *Think, Phoebe, think.* In that brief moment of near-lucidity two weeks ago, Frances mentioned something *catching* as someone rushed by her or at her. Who was that person? Vincent? An intruder intent on robbery? Craig, the former teacher? Surely not Craig. Who else might have been on the grounds that Thursday night? Caspar had left rehearsal early for his Catholic fundraiser. Doug, the associate director, had finished the rehearsal but then rushed off, according to Caspar. Doug, brilliant English musician, married with two children: hardly a suspicious character, and like everyone there, already questioned by the police. The clergy. The clergy were all there—or were they? I realized that in my private talks with Fathers Bakewell, Blum, and Sauer, I had not actually asked them exactly where they had been and what they had been doing that night! How could I have? That would have been too pointed. Father Blum was the one who discovered Claire slumped on the path, and he had rushed to the rectory to tell Father Bakewell and call the police. So those two were around. But Father Sauer? Where was Father Sauer that night? I wracked my memory of our talk on the park bench: no, I didn't recall any mention of where he had been that night. But again, the police would have examined him, too, so apparently all of the clergy were beyond suspicion.

Still, as I walked, I decided I must try to talk again with Father Bakewell, and with the music director Averill Page, whom I had not even met yet, away as he had been in Germany. I decided I would try to speak with Averill after the service on Sunday and see whether today I could see Father Bakewell one more time.

I arrived at Saint Bede's at 10:00, but instead of going to the rectory decided to go into the church to sit and ponder for a moment. I entered through the south side door. I sank into a pew in the dimly lit old nave and gazed up at the beautiful stained-glass windows. How pleasant it was to sit in quiet, empty churches, I mused. *The quieter and emptier, the better.* After only about three minutes, I heard someone enter from the side door. I glanced to my right, and who should that be but Averill Page! I rose and walked towards him.

"Excuse me, sorry, I'm Phoebe Overbridge, Frances's sister. I don't think we've met, but you are Averill Page, the music director, I think?"

He stopped abruptly in his stride, eyebrows raised and lips parted in surprise. This was the first time I'd seen him in street clothes rather than in service cassock and surplice. Of medium-short stature and stocky build with thinning wavy brown hair combed straight back in a fashionably arty way, he was wearing trim black trousers and a dapper royal-blue short-sleeved shirt and had several scores in hand.

"I didn't mean to burst in on you, very sorry! I actually thought I might see if Father Bakewell was in, and I was just pausing a few minutes here in your beautiful space."

Recovering his calm and poise, he replied, "Yes, I'm Averill Page. Phoebe, good to meet you, and I am so very, very sorry about what happened here a few weeks ago. We are all simply devastated."

"Devastated" seemed to the be the adjective of choice among *all* the staff here in this context, I thought to myself.

"I asked our Caspar to visit Frances at the hospital on behalf of all of us, and I believe he did."

"Yes, he did, a couple weeks ago. I was there, too, when he came, and we talked for a while. Such a kind young man."

Averill's eyes lit up and then darted away briefly from my gaze. "My student. A unique young man. Our assistant choirmaster. I've come to depend on him."

I nodded warmly and studied Averill's face carefully at this point. It was quietly glowing. He was obviously quite fond of Caspar—that was clear. And perhaps rather possessive? What had Victor described about Averill inviting Caspar out for drinks? And Frances, in an email—had Averill eyed her once in a strange way? My thoughts began to swim and a wild idea entered my head. Could Averill have observed the rather playful and affectionate friendship that had sprung up between Caspar and Frances and, smitten with jealousy, taken a dislike to her?

"How is Frances?" Averill asked evenly, looking directly at me, his hazel eyes neutral and intense.

"She is still unconscious," I replied, stopping myself just in time from adding *but starting to mumble things from time to time.* "But the doctor assures me there is hope."

Averill nodded sympathetically.

Visualizing Frances immobile and supine in her lonely white hospital bed, I suddenly felt a bit weak-kneed. I asked, "Would you have just a few minutes to sit down and talk with me right now, Averill? It would mean a lot to me…"

"Of course." He had about thirty minutes before he had to leave for a rehearsal downtown. I put a steadying hand on the polished wooden pew back in front of me and sat down slowly, as Averill seated himself smoothly next to me.

"First, let me say, your services here are just beautiful," I began, deciding to take as winning an approach as possible. "I've attended twice now, and Frances writes me lots of emails about how much she loves the chorus."

Averill smiled and the muscles around his eyes visibly relaxed. "We work hard at the liturgy here. Traditional sermons and prayers can sustain some people, but many, especially in these anxiety-producing times, aren't really reached that way. That's where excellent sacred music comes in: it moves the heart strings, you know? It comforts and lifts our spirits in a very deep way."

My eyes brightened and I nodded in agreement. "I love the old Anglican and classical pieces."

"We program a mix of basically everything here," Averill was quick to point out. "Not just the traditional Anglican fare, lovely though it is. This is a very diverse neighborhood, as you may have noticed. We want to draw in as many people as possible. Which means we must include black spirituals, Hispanic songs, even some Asian pieces."

"I see."

"Yes, it's important. We can't leave anyone behind. Young people today are not exposed to the classics as much as we older folks were growing up. Too often they seem unmoved by the classics."

"That's a pity."

"Yes…but it's the reality. We have to *go with the flow,* as it were, to keep attendance up here."

"I've heard that church attendance in the country in general is down…"

"Not in the mega-churches, the really evangelical, Bible-thumping sorts. But we are not that here at Saint Bede's. We can never be that, much as…well, much as there *are* some positive aspects to all that. The Anglican-Episcopal tradition simply generally does not function that way."

"With a lot of fervor, you mean? Strong *come-to-Jesus* sort of preaching? Altar calls?"

Averill emitted a short laugh. "Right. In fact, among the denominations, we are sometimes called 'God's frozen people,'"—I smiled—"which is a shame. We are supposed to be the most moderate, reasonable, *via-media* of all the churches, but what happens too often, I think, is that liturgies and sermons simply bog down. Not enough zip, passion, energy."

"I see your point."

"I'm glad you do."

"I suppose not everyone agrees, of course," I added.

Averill's eyes narrowed for an instant but he quickly resumed his pleasant manner. "Naturally. People never agree one hundred percent. Here or anywhere else."

"The joys and hazards of human civilization," I murmured.

"We try to keep our arguments civil here," he said, but a cloud had clearly crossed his face.

I decided to take my chances. I softly asked, "Could any argument you know of have played a role in what happened to Frances? Is she well liked as a chorus member? I mean, do you know of any friction she might have been having with anyone here?"

Averill's eyes narrowed almost imperceptibly once again and he took a small, sharp intake of breath. "Of course Frances is well liked. I mean, I do not rehearse the chorus—that is the task of Caspar and Doug—but when the pro choir and the chorus combine to sing a service, I've always found Frances to be a friendly person, attentive singer, and everyone seems to get along very well." As Averill pronounced these positive words, his face nevertheless seemed masklike. He went on. "Frances just joined us last fall, as you know. A lovely woman." He then looked directly at me and smiled warmly. "We are fond of all our singers here, a good environment."

I knew from my various conversations with Saint Bede's people that this was, quite simply, not the whole truth. I asked very softly, "So, no…irritating incompatibilities or rivalries that you know of?"

Averill remained silent and looked down at his strong and supple organist's hands folded in his lap. Stillness filled the church, mid-morning light streaming through the windows created colorful mosaics on the far walls and pillars, and neither of us spoke. Averill swallowed audibly.

"I am sorry to ask such a question," I murmured. "But as you can imagine…"

"Of course, of course," he responded, falling silent again. "No," he said at last. "No. We have the usual sorts of drama here that most churches have, I'll tell you that. Budding romances among the singers, competition for solos, criticism from the ranks that springs up at times. But it's a good group of people here at Saint Bede's. I mean, everyone *means well.* We try to work together harmoniously. We have our differences, but…no. Certainly no one here is at all inclined to violence, if that is what you mean."

"That *would* be surprising."

"The police spent over a week questioning every staff member here. Everyone was elsewhere at the time that Claire met her death, and one can only assume the guilty person also encountered Frances as he—or she—fled the grounds. I myself was with the rector and Father Sauer. That evening—it was a Thursday, I recall—August held an early working dinner at the rectory to discuss music and liturgy for the coming year. Then we all got in a cab and went to Lincoln Center, the Met. *Tosca.* A gift from one of our generous donors here."

"Oh, I see. *Tosca!* One of the few operas I've seen—a PBS special I watched just a couple months ago! Now *there* is some church drama for you," I mused. "Doesn't the diva stab the evil baron to death in the church and then place a crucifix on his chest?"

"Not in the church, my dear," corrected Averill with slight irritation in his tone. "In his private quarters. She stabs him in his apartment."

"Very grisly, in any case."

"Yes, indeed. Phoebe, apologies, but my rehearsal downtown beckons. I'm sorry not to have been of any help to you, and I really am just as in the dark as everyone else here as to what happened to those two very lovely young women."

I nodded, realizing I had learned nothing new in this conversation except that the clergy and

Averill had attended an opera the evening of April 22.

"Thank you for talking with me, Averill. I'm sure they will figure it all out soon."

The music director shook my hand warmly and then briskly exited the pew and strode to the south door, where he disappeared, leaving me to sit alone once more in the silent church. Precisely nothing gained there, I mused. All the clergy at dinner at the rectory and then off to the opera. Except…*wait!* Averill did not mention Father Blum's presence at the dinner or opera! And he was the one who discovered Frances later that night and rushed to tell Father Bakewell at the rectory. Discovered or… I shuddered. Father Blum had seemed so genuine in our talk, and yet, could I finally be on to something here?

I quickly rose and exited the quiet, empty church, which had suddenly begun to feel not at all pleasant but in fact very oppressive.

11 ✠ May 15

Frances has awakened! I was at my usual morning place beside her bed today, listening to *Peer Gynt* on the radio and scheming as to how I was going to arrange to talk with Father Blum again, when Frances *spoke.* My gaze flew to her face. Her eyes were open and alert and she asked, "What time is it? Where am I?"

"You're awake! Oh, my goodness…"

She looked at me serenely and repeated, "Where am I?"

"Oh, my dear Frances, in the hospital. You've been out for over three weeks. This is tremendous!"

She smiled faintly and stretched her arms, which had grown quite thin, lightly to each side. I was afraid she might immediately fade out again and so said quickly, "How do you feel? How are you?"

"Fine. I feel fine. How very strange. How did I get here?"

Torn between immediately running to alert the nurse and continuing to talk with Frances, I elected the latter. "My dear, they found you at church, Saint Bede's. You'd apparently fallen, hit your head. A concussion."

"Really?"

"Yes." I went on carefully, not wanting to put thoughts into her head but rather hear what she might remember. "Do you remember falling?"

At that moment, the nurse Violet came into the room. I cried, "She's awake! Can you believe it? Look, see!"

Violet smiled with true joy and said, "This is wonderful! I'll page Dr. Lasso right now." And she disappeared down the hall.

"You said…how long was I asleep?" asked Frances.

"From the night of April 22 until just now. Just over three weeks."

Her eyes widened and her brow furrowed. "I'm very thirsty," she murmured.

I sprang up to get her a glass of water. "You're hooked up to fluids, dear—they've been feeding you that way—so don't worry. You're fine. I'll just go ask the nurse if it's okay for you to drink now."

I worried that in my short absence to fetch water, Frances might sink back into the darkness. How desperate I felt to begin asking her a hundred probing questions!

Nurse Violet and I reentered the room, Violet with a pink pitcher of water and a plastic cup. To our joy, Frances was still awake, her beautiful brown eyes looking up expectantly at us and her hands now clasped at her chest.

"I'm going to raise the head of the bed a little so you can sit up more to drink," said Violet as she grasped the electronic remote. "You must take *small* sips," she instructed, adjusting Frances's pillows. "You haven't eaten for a few weeks, and your stomach can handle only small quantities right now. Small sips, dear." She turned to me and said, "Dr. Lasso is *thrilled.* He will be here as soon as he can."

Frances obediently took two small sips of water and murmured, "Mmm." I could not help smiling from ear to ear. Violet disappeared once more.

"So I fell at church?" she asked with a puzzled expression.

I pulled my chair closer to her and said, "Yes. After rehearsal. It was a Thursday night. One of the priests found you, they told me. They called an ambulance, they rushed you here. You've been out like a light until just now." I could not bear to tell her yet about Claire.

"Amazing! I don't remember anything."

"What is the last thing you remember?" I asked, wondering whether she would repeat her comment of a couple weeks prior that something had *caught.*

"I remember," she began and then paused for a big yawn. "Let's see, I remember being at rehearsal. I walked into the rehearsal hall and saw Caspar in a chic black blazer sitting in my soprano chair, chatting with Georgina and Zoe. He looked so charming and animated. As I walked towards the soprano section, he looked up and we made eye contact, big smiles. 'Welcome back!' I said, as he'd been away in Mexico the week before at some family wedding. He jumped up and cried, 'Frances!' and gave me a big warm hug. 'I liked your art photos,' I remember telling him. He'd taken an excursion, on his own, after the wedding. I marveled that even in the poorest parts of all countries people found expression through art—in this case, Caspar had taken photos of several huge colorful murals along rather dilapidated streets. He responded, 'Yes, heroic and inspiring, isn't it!' You know how lavishly he tends to phrase things, Phoebe," remarked Frances with a big smile. "Then I asked, had everything gone well, the wedding, the family events? Yes, wonderfully. He'd flown back just the night before. I commented, 'Oh! Jet lag!' 'Not really,' Caspar said. 'A long flight, but just one time zone off New York time,' and of course as he said that I realized it, too. 'Yes, of course—I knew that. I love maps!' I cried. *'I do, too!'* Caspar replied warmly, his face lighting up. I said I could look at maps all day long."

It was heartening to see Frances so delighted in this recollection of the rehearsal, although I was not sure how relevant any of these observations would be. But I just smiled encouragingly and let her ramble on.

"Oh! Caspar said that the murals photos were not from their town but from a town about two hours north via bus. I said yes, I knew they lived in Puebla, and he'd labeled the photos as from Tampico. 'You'd gone off exploring, I figured, a day trip.' Then he said this adorable thing: 'When I was walking around there, I thought to myself, *Frances is going to lecture me about traveling in dangerous places!*' Well, Phoebe, I found that so endearing that I turned away for a minute to put my jacket on the back of the chair, realizing I was smiling with secret elation that Caspar should say such a thing, as if I were his big sister or…some such. I murmured with mock-aloofness, 'I don't do that anymore, my dear,' meaning lecture him, but as I turned back to him, no doubt with a beaming face despite myself, he repeated with a slightly over-excited mien, *'Frances is going to lecture me about traveling in dangerous places!!'* I smiled, facing him, rather in wonder, shook my head gently, and then had the brilliance to say, with one index finger raised, 'But I'm glad you're *thinking* that way. You do need to be *very careful!*'"

Frances laughed merrily and continued. "He was delighted. I really think he just loves any hint of a mother's sort of touch, that kind of solicitous concern for his welfare."

I said to her, "You and Caspar are sweet, you really are. I've told you that before."

"Yes! Pity about the big age difference, and other differences as well, but I agree—we enjoy a strange, sweet affinity."

"What else do you remember about that evening?"

"Let's see. Oh, I remember that Caspar also said that although it wasn't a matter of jet lag, he had gotten in very late and hadn't been able to sleep! I commented that sleep was not so much about physical fatigue, was it, but really about the state of the mind. I told him I had that racing-mind problem, too, sometimes."

"Two peas in a pod, you two."

"Stop it."

We laughed.

"He also told me that he'd spoken in Spanish the whole time he'd been there, and I'd said, '*¡Qué bien!*'"

"More motherly positive reinforcement," I joked.

"Yes!" said Frances with a broad grin. "There was one more funny moment. Before the guys warm us up vocally at the piano, they sometimes have us do backrubs. 'Turn left, everyone. Back rubs!' So as we were doing that, Georgina, giving me my rub, remarked, 'I'll be gentle.' I said, 'Well, it's just that I'm mostly skin and bones.' I noticed that Caspar was sort of listening in. Georgina then said, 'Yes, you are delicate.' Caspar quipped dryly, '*Delicate!*' I turned my head to him with a look of amusement and almost blushed, I think. Maybe he was thinking of some of our hugs when I've come in to rehearsal having had a glass of wine with dinner. I guess really I am pretty strong."

"You are simply hilarious, you two!"

"Oh," she continued, her smile suddenly fading. "I remember that as all this was going on, this entertaining banter with Caspar, I suddenly looked over and noticed a couple of the staff had come in, Averill Page, the music director, and Father Blum—have I mentioned him, the pastoral care priest?"

I just nodded. There would be time later to tell Frances all about my recent face-to-face acquaintances made at Saint Bede's. I waited, eager to hear the suite.

"They seemed to be glaring at me!"

"*Glaring* at you?"

"Yes!"

"Are you sure? But why?"

"No idea. They seemed to be glaring at *me,* but maybe as I think about it now, they were glaring at Caspar, who was standing quite close to me. Or at both of us! It was just a brief sort of thing, but I definitely got a strange feeling. Too much hilarity, maybe?"

My pulse quickened. "Why were they there? They don't usually show up at chorus rehearsals, do they?"

"No, never, or at least never Father Blum. In fact, they had come to announce something. Everyone stopped the back rubs and faced them, and then Averill told us somberly that one of our very generous music program donors, Mrs. Alodia Greyling, had collapsed earlier that day and been taken to the hospital. A massive stroke, apparently. Her life was hanging by a thread, he said, and he wanted us all to keep her very much in our prayers. He added that Mrs. Greyling, in her seventies, had been a member of Saint Bede's for upwards of forty years and had, some years, almost single-handedly kept the music program going through her incredible generosity. Of course, we all felt stunned and very sorry, and the room was dead quiet."

"Understandable. That is sad."

"Averill—who seemed a little overly emotive to me, but then, I don't really know him very well—went on for a few minutes about wonderful, special Mrs. Greyling and that, in fact, it was she who had given a recent gift to the staff, three tickets to a Metropolitan Opera production for that very night—I think it was *Tosca.*"

I blinked a few times and nodded.

"They were not going to waste the tickets, he said, but go ahead and attend. I think he said that three of them were going. Father Blum then said that he would not be attending, would be in his quarters that evening, if anyone needed or wanted to stop by. 'Alodia Greyling is a very, very dear person,' he remarked quietly. 'And she is a widow with no children. Please do keep her in your prayers, and if you happen to know her personally, as many of us here do, of course, please consider paying her a visit at the hospital, Saint Raphael's, just down the street. We hope she is not going to leave us just yet.'"

As I sat listening to my suddenly, miraculously voluble sister, I realized that here indeed was confirmation that Father Blum had not attended the opera on the tragic evening of April 22. And I wondered whether poor Mrs. Greyling was still hospitalized, right here, on another floor, or had moved on to a completely new realm.

"Well, that must have been a sad way to start rehearsal. Rehearsal went on, I assume?"

"Yes, it did. Before Averill and Father Blum left, I noticed again that they glanced over towards me, or Caspar, with unpleasant-looking faces. Maybe I'm exaggerating this now in my mind, I don't know. Or maybe I was just seeing their somberness and worry over Mrs. Greyling. Probably."

I remained silent with various thoughts whirling, whirling.

"Oh, and Caspar left mid-way through for some reason, and Doug led the rehearsal for the last hour or so."

"Hmm. Then—after rehearsal? Did you leave the hall as you usually do?" I very much wanted to remind her that she had once murmured a few words on this subject, but I did not.

Frances pondered silently for a good moment. Finally, she said, "I have no memory at all of leaving the hall."

12 ✠ May 16

It is Sunday today. I have told my poor sister that her fellow singer Claire was found dead inside the church hall the morning of April 23. She cried for a solid hour as I sat holding her hand.

They will keep Frances in the hospital for a few more days, verifying her muscular strength and balance and her ability to handle regular food. She's been on clear liquids only, will advance to puddings and that sort of thing, and finally to solid food. When her gut is fully capable of digesting that, all else being well, she'll at last be discharged. She's had a slight headache ever since she awoke yesterday, and Dr. Lasso is going to evaluate that. The tragic news about Claire has now obviously brought her very low.

Detective Morales is going to come to question her tomorrow.

I sat with her most the morning until she was calmer and told her I would return in the afternoon for a longer visit. I am not sure why I did not tell her that I was going to attend Saint Bede's at 11:00, but I didn't. After all, I haven't told her yet what a sleuth I've been these last weeks, all the tête-à-têtes I've had with Saint

Bede's folk. I resolved to tell her all about those soon and yearned to have some truly key insight to share. More on that later.

So off I trudged to Saint Bede's at 10:30, determined to talk again with the clergy. At 11:00 precisely, the little bell rang, the hymn introduction flooded out from the organ, those who could began to sing, and I watched the company in its full glory—minus, of course, the community chorus—process in and past me: the crucifer with his immense bronze cross flanked by his white-clad, candle-bearing acolytes; Caspar, the children, on duty today with the professional singers, Averill, all garbed in their cranberry-colored cassocks and white surplices; and Fathers Sauer, Blum, and Bakewell, in their shiny priestly vestments with silken stoles. I discreetly looked around the congregation and spotted Everild off to the right and Craig in his usual far-left seat.

It was a long service, with a very long sung psalm, three anthems, and a scholarly sermon by Father Sauer about Caroline Chisholm, a little-known English woman of the nineteenth century who had devoted most of her life to the welfare of female immigrants in Australia and whose saintly efforts had also come to the attention of the great novelist Charles Dickens. The sermon began well, I thought, with lots of interesting historical information, but at the fifteen-minute mark, Father Sauer launched into Part Two, relating Chisholm's actions to current immigration problems and policy in America, and the whole thing then went on for *another* fifteen minutes. Valuable as all this no doubt was, most everyone present began to show signs of restlessness, especially given the stuffy air in the church on this unusually warm May day and Father Sauer's rather dry preaching style. I observed singers and congregants discreetly fanning themselves and exchanging a few impatient glances. The children fidgeted, despite periodic stern glances from Caspar. On top of all this, once the service finally moved on to communion, the incense was used liberally, which, on such a warm day, seemed to cause quite a few eruptions of coughing, not only among the singers but also among those in the congregation seated in the front few pews. I remembered Vincent's complaints and glanced to check his reaction: he was using his black music folder in a somewhat less than subtle way to deflect the scented smoke.

In any case, the service finally ended at about 12:20, and I got straight in line to greet the rector. As I reached him, I saw his eyes widen ever so slightly, as if he were surprised to see me there *yet again,* but he smiled, greeted me by name, and shook my hand. He then quickly looked beyond me to the next person in line, but I said quietly and with focus, "Father Bakewell, I wanted you to know that Frances has finally woken up." His eyebrows shot up as his gaze returned to me, and then he smiled serenely and said, "Well, praise God! Now that is very good news. And she is well?" I said yes, very, and apologetically asked whether he could once again spare just a few minutes to talk with me. Of course he could.

Fifteen minutes later, seated once more in his cozy rectory parlor with a lemonade at my side, I told Father Bakewell how it had unfolded Saturday morning.

"So it was Edvard Grieg who had the honor of bringing her round, then? I never underestimate the power of music, you know, quite seriously."

"No doubt," I remarked. "On that score, Frances recalls quite well everything that happened during the chorus rehearsal the night of the…incidents. But her mind is still a blank as to how she fell afterwards."

"I see."

"She said that Averill and Father Blum had paid a visit to the group, with the news about your generous donor, poor Mrs. Greyling."

"Yes, poor Alodia, but she's made a near-full recovery now, somewhat miraculously. She's home once more, a niece staying with her temporarily. She's a resilient old soul, I must say, God bless her."

"Oh, I am glad to hear that! She must have been cared for in a room right there in Saint Raphael's not far from Frances. Well, Averill shared with the chorus that Mrs. Greyling had given you clergy tickets to the opera and that not to waste them—and of course you would already have paid her a visit at the hospital (I did not actually know this but heard myself say it!)—you attended."

Father Bakewell frowned almost imperceptibly. "Yes, that is so," he said. "Was it *Turandot*, I think…"

"*Tosca,* apparently."

"Of course, yes, it was *Tosca.*"

At that moment Father Blum appeared at the door. "Pardon me, but I heard Phoebe was here and I just wondered…"

I said immediately, "Oh please, do join us. I was just telling Father Bakewell the good news about Frances finally waking up. She's alert and well!" My mind began whirling as I wondered how on earth I could probe Father Blum's possible involvement in the sad events of April 22 with that very man now joining our company!

"I am thrilled beyond words, my dear Phoebe," said Father Blum with real warmth. "Our prayers have been answered."

"Yes. Her memory seems remarkably intact, except, unfortunately, for how she ended up collapsed on the path that night. She was utterly crushed to hear about Claire. I told her just this morning, before church. She cried for an hour straight."

Father Bakewell shook his head sadly as Father Blum pulled a small armchair closer to us and sat down.

"Phoebe was just mentioning the opera we attended the night of April 22," said Father Bakewell.

"*Turandot,* wasn't it?"

"*Tosca,*" the rector corrected.

"Ah. Averill and Fathers Bakewell and Sauer are huge opera fans, unlike myself, I must admit. I find the plots often too melodramatic. Pity about Averill's indisposition, however."

"I beg your pardon?" I asked.

Father Bakewell shot a stern glance at Father Blum but responded simply, "Something he ate. He was fine."

"Averill was not well that night?" I pursued.

"He apparently had some stomach distress about an hour into the opera," said Father Bakewell. "We'd had a working dinner that evening here at the rectory, a bit rushed, you know, and then dashed off to the Met—"

"After Averill and Father Blum had called in on the chorus?" I interrupted.

"Yes…that must be right. We took a taxi at about 7:00—the performance started at 7:30."

I knew that the chorus rehearsal began at 7:00, so to this point everything Father Bakewell was relating seemed to fit into the time framework Frances had described.

"As I recall, it was just at the start of the *Te Deum* near the end of Act 1 that Averill got up and left the box. He'd put a hand to his abdomen and made a slightly sour face and whispered, 'Excuse me.'"

"And he came back?"

Father Bakewell remained silent for a few seconds too long, it felt.

"He did not."

"So…he…?"

"We were a bit worried. At the intermission after Act 1, we went to the bar area on that level looking for him, and a few minutes later Father Sauer, who'd had the wisdom to bring his fancy phone, received a text from Averill saying he'd gone home by cab."

"He'd gone home," I heard myself repeat quietly. Averill would have been back on the church grounds by about 9:00, I reflected, just the time that chorus rehearsal would be ending. In our chat, Averill had mentioned to me that they had gone to the opera that evening, but had uttered not a word about his early departure from it.

"Yes, home," said Father Bakewell. "And straight to bed, apparently, understandably."

"I see," I murmured, trying to process this brand-new piece of information and what it might imply. And yet, I pondered, Father Blum had been at home *all evening:* now both he and Averill were established as being on the grounds around the times, it seemed, that Claire had met her end and Frances had fallen.

I looked to Father Blum and asked, "You saw Averill arrive back at the church grounds?"

Father Blum looked down to study the mock-Persian carpet, then shifted his gaze briefly to a bas-relief wall sculpture in steel and bronze of Christ in Agony, and then looked directly into my eyes.

"No," he said. "I can't say I saw him return, as such. But my apartment has a partial view of the main avenue, as well as of the courtyard, and just before 9:00, I would say, glancing out my window, seated at my desk, I do recall seeing a yellow cab pull up. The entrance drive itself to our grounds is a ways up and out of sight, so I don't know who got out—or got in, for that matter."

"But Averill's apartment is not far from yours, I believe? Did you hear him come in?"

"His apartment is in this wing, yes, but I can't say that I heard him at any point. I was reviewing my notes on a pastoral care client of mine whom I was meeting in the morning. I don't normally spy on my neighbors or have any inclination to do so, you know."

"No, of course not, I realize that," I said quickly. "I'm just curious…"

Father Bakewell said, "I saw Averill in the morning, as we clergy and music staff often attend morning prayer together at 7:30, and I asked him how he was. He did look pale, and he reported that he'd felt queasy after eating the *pasta primavera alfredo* the night before at our working dinner—he said sometimes various cheeses didn't agree with him—but had gone ahead to the opera thinking he would shake it off. Averill does like his wine, too, you know, a jolly sort of soul, and well—I think we'd had a Tenuta le Calcinaie Vernaccia that evening, one of Averill's favorites, and in sum, these instances of indigestion happen to everyone."

"Of course they do," echoed Father Blum.

"Indeed," I agreed, trying to disguise my discomfort with the degree of *luxe et volupté* I was sensing at the clerical tables of Saint Bede's and remembering what Craig Scranch had said about the lavish sort of catering that went on there.

Father Bakewell went on. "Averill apologized for having had to leave the opera in mid-stream. He commented that he'd taken some Pepto Bismol, I think it was, and gone to bed, not slept particularly well—in fact, he looked pretty raw, I have to say, that next morning—but that he was fine, or would be fine."

I knew I was treading on extremely thin ground here, and of course there really was no reason to suspect anyone at all on the staff of Saint Bede's of having committed the horrific incidents of that April night. And to imply that I suspected any of them would clearly not work to my advantage. I quickly changed tack and said, "I was just thinking that since Averill apparently was crossing the courtyard just at the time, or thereabouts, that chorus rehearsal was ending, he would have been ideally placed to have noticed any stranger on the grounds, anyone lingering around there who shouldn't have been."

"True!" said Father Bakewell.

"Yes!" said Father Blum.

"But I suppose the police have been over all that with him in their questioning."

"No doubt," said Father Bakewell as Father Blum nodded reflectively, silently.

"Father Blum, we know that you found Frances slumped on the path that night as you were heading back to the church for your book…"

"Yes, my dear, we've been over all that. That was much later, about 10:20 or so, I think. There was not a soul around that I could see, nor would you expect anyone to be there at that hour, of course."

I was hitting dead ends again, I realized, and the tension in the room had increased palpably.

At that point, a knock came on the door and Father Bakewell, looking relieved, rose, with a quick steadying hand on the side of his desk, saying, "Excuse me."

Everild was there with two men in light brown maintenance uniforms. "Sorry, Father," she said, "but Dave and Delroy have found an unusual number of mice in the hall area just now. All right to call the exterminator on Monday?"

"Goodness. Yes, of course," said the rector, and the trio began to withdraw down the hall. But Father Bakewell called one of them back. "Delroy, may I ask for five minutes of your time? Please come in."

Delroy, a tall, strong, heavy black man with a dark blue-green leaf-and-branch-patterned tattoo on one forearm in the middle of which read *Jesus Saves,* walked in shyly. "Yes, Father?" He stood with his weight more on one leg than the other and with his hands clasped in front of himself.

"Delroy, I believe it was you who came across Claire's body that terrible morning a few weeks ago, correct?"

"Yes, Father, that was me." He spoke with a lilting Jamaican accent.

"In the basement hall."

"Yes, sir, near the big piano."

"Yes." Then, remaining standing and gently extending a thin, bony hand in my direction, he said, "Delroy, this is Phoebe, Frances's sister. You know Frances was the other woman who was found collapsed, but up on the pathway leading out of the church."

"Ma'am," said Delroy with a nod of the head. "I'm very sorry, ma'am."

"Thank you. She's now finally getting better."

Delroy's serious expression did not change as he said, "I am glad to hear that, ma'am."

"Delroy is one of our excellent maintenance staff, along with Dave and two others."

I nodded appreciatively.

Father Bakewell continued, addressing Delroy squarely. "We are all still puzzling over what exactly happened that night, how Claire and Frances fell, whether an intruder entered and if so, *why, to what purpose.* Delroy, please think very carefully. What do you remember about the scene right when you discovered Claire's body in the hall?"

"Everything was just the same as always, Father—except for the body. I couldn't believe it, you know? She was face down, her hair splayed out, her arms mostly underneath her."

"Trying to cushion her fall, I suppose."

"I don't know, sir, but she was a fright to see for sure, poor thing."

"The room, the floor, Delroy, anything at all about the place that you remember that could be of help?"

"As I said, sir—well, as I was turning to run out to tell you, I remember now that I slid a little bit."

"Slid?"

"My left leg is still a little unsteady, you know, Father, from the accident last year. I must have turned too fast. A slick spot, sir. I glanced down, something a little white and green…"

"What on earth…an insect?"

"Maybe food, sir."

"Delroy, I don't follow you. How food? The chorus rehearsals never include food, as far as I am aware."

"No, sir, but Cedric brings leftovers sometimes to the fridge there for the soup kitchen, to serve to the guests on Saturday. Maybe it was a little spinach, or broccoli…"

"Leftovers from *where?*"

"I am sorry, Father, if you haven't known about this." Delroy looked nervous and shifted back and forth on his legs and squeezed his large, strong hands together at his chest. "Leftovers from some of the suppers you fathers have at the rectory, mostly the ones that are catered."

Father Bakewell's eyebrows shot up in surprise, and Father Blum let out a little laugh and murmured, "*Pasta primavera*, August, it must have been a bit of *pasta primavera* on the floor."

Father Bakewell glared at Father Blum. "Did you know about this, Martyn?"

"I'm afraid I learned about it just two weeks or so ago, but I've kept the knowledge to myself…not wanting to upset you, August. But really, why not? There's no reason to waste food. Why not serve it to our soup-kitchen guests, after all? It can only be a very little bit, in the grand outlay we make for meal supplies, after all."

"Well, I suppose so," mused Father Bakewell. "But if some guests, maybe the first in line, get a serving of, well shrimp cocktail or braised asparagus, and…"

"Didn't we have stuffed Florentine mushrooms the other night, when we hosted the Australian bishop, what was his name…"

"Ragdale."

"Yes, old Ragdale."

"…and others *don't,* word could get out. I mean, we must treat all our guests equally…"

I intervened impatiently. "But the point is, pardon me, it seems that Cedric could have been in the hall just around the time that Claire…went down."

We all remained awkwardly silent for a good ten seconds, each no doubt stewing hotly in the depths of his or her own mind and struggling with what to say next.

Father Bakewell looked unwaveringly at the maintenance man and asked, "Delroy, when you were questioned by the police, did you tell them about sliding on the green-and-white…blob?"

"No, sir, I only just remembered that now."

We all held our breath and looked at Delroy.

Father Bakewell went on. "Delroy, think very carefully: do you recall seeing Cedric around the hall that morning, or the night before?"

Delroy shifted back and forth on his legs once more, raised his head skyward briefly, looked down at his solid rubber-soled shoes, and then shook his head slightly. "I really can't remember, Father Bakewell," he said finally. "It was, what, several weeks ago now? That particular night…what day of the week was that, sir?"

"A Thursday. Chorus rehearsal night."

"Thursday. Thursday," Delroy repeated, rubbing his chin.

"Also, three of us staff had gone out to the opera after our working dinner."

Delroy shook his head and looked vacant. "I work the morning shift on Thursdays and Fridays, sir. Eight to three. Dave does three to ten. He must have checked the church doors that night, sir. Unless he was off that day and it was Alwin or Todd. I don't remember exactly, sir. I just remember finding her at about 8:15 in the morning—it would have been a Friday morning, then—as I was going down to mop the hall. I am sorry, sir."

"Don't be sorry, Delroy. You've perhaps added a piece to the puzzle," I murmured.

Father Bakewell sighed heavily with a hand to his downcast forehead and said, "Thank you, Delroy, for your time." Delroy bowed his head slightly and quickly left the parlor.

Once the door was closed again, I said to the two priests, "We have to talk with Dave and Cedric."

"Everyone has been thoroughly questioned by the police, my dear," said Father Bakewell in a tone of exhaustion, taking a seat once more. "None of our staff saw Claire's body upon lock-up that night: that has been firmly established. Of course, they do not normally do a thorough check of the hall, either—why would they? Nothing like this has ever happened in the history of Saint Bede's."

"Understandable, but this possibility of food spilled on the floor—that is new. It may be nothing, but it may be something. We could call Detective Morales…"

"No," said Father Bakewell. "This is quite irrelevant, some little crumb or leaf that might have been on the ground—I really don't see the point."

"He's right," said Father Blum. "No doubt completely meaningless."

I gulped, surprised by their reactions. Once more I knew that I had to back off or risk offending these churchmen, on whom I depended for information and access to this shadowy world of Saint Bede's. So I said, "I suppose so, after all. Since everyone has been questioned already. True. Yet we are still completely in the dark."

"Yes, we are," said Father Bakewell, looking seriously into my eyes as we all rose to depart.

As I thanked the priests cordially and bid them good-bye, I felt renewed anguish and discouragement. But I also resolved that I would somehow find a way to talk with Dave and Cedric.

*

As I walked slowly down the drive leaving the Saint Bede's grounds, a young woman ran up behind me and said, slightly out of breath, "Oh hello, sorry to bother you like this, but I think you are Frances's sister?"

I turned and recognized one of the singers on whose conversation in the Café Lyonnais I had eavesdropped only three days ago! *Oh, dear.* "Yes, I'm Phoebe Overbridge."

"I'm Rowena Plink. I'm an alto in the pro choir." Facing me was a slim young woman with long blond hair looking very serious and earnest.

We looked each other full in the face, which we had never done before, and I sensed that she did not recognize me from the café. I felt relieved. "Oh, I see. Very nice to meet you…"

"I've seen you at our services and found out today who you are. May I please talk with you? It's rather urgent."

I felt a surge of excitement as I said, "Of course. I'd be only too happy. Where shall we go?"

Rowena glanced around for a moment with slight confusion and then said, "Let's just walk for a while. Let's walk uptown."

As we turned right out of the church drive, she said, "Actually, let's head over to the park."

"Fine." I silently recalled sitting in the park not so many days ago with Father Radcliffe Sauer. I hoped this conversation would be as lively and informative.

Just as we were about to cross the avenue, a man in a black jacket, torn jeans, and heavy black boots riding a very loud motorcycle roared through the yellow light at terrifying speed. As he shot by, a grey-bearded man about to step off the curb shouted, "Get a muffler, you moron!" The motorcyclist swerved very slightly and stuck his right hand out in a rude gesture. The old man shouted again, *"Idiot!"* but the biker was far up the avenue by that time.

"I hate New York," said Rowena as we looked carefully both ways and began to cross.

"I've often wondered exactly why Frances decided to move here," I said. "I mean, I do understand about the wealth of art and culture here, but on the other hand..."

"It's not worth it, after all," the alto said flatly. "I've been here now for about four years, from North Carolina. I was all aglow when I first arrived. I attended the School of the Arts in

Winston-Salem, majored in voice, came up here for a workshop, and then on a whim decided to audition for the Saint Bede's Choir—and got in! I was tickled pink! That was then…"

"The choir sounds very nice, by the way," I remarked. "I've attended three Sunday services now, and you all sound wonderful."

"Thank you. But it's not what it seems, all that beauty and peace and etherealness."

"How so?"

"The subtle cut-throat competitive vibe among the choir. We're all soloists, you know, and this is a paid job for us. I happen to be a believer, I take communion, but I'm the only pro who does. I'm not at all saying they are *bad* people, not at all, but they are there strictly for the music. And Averill seems to favor some of us over others. Some people get more solos than others, more eye contact, more positive comments."

"Sorry to hear it," I said softly.

"I remember my mother saying to me periodically back when I was in high school and starting to think about majoring in music in college: 'If you really love an art form, don't make it your job.' I found that horrific! *Jane,'* I would respond with the sharp irritation of sixteen, seventeen years old—my brother and I always call her by her first name, but that's another story—'that is *ridiculous.* We all know we should *follow our bliss!* Why do you say that?' She would reply, 'I don't mean to clip your wings, dear'—isn't that cute? She always said *I don't mean to clip your wings*—'but beautiful as the art world is, it is cut-throat. It is a world of beautiful deception. And you are judged constantly: by the directors, the producers, other artists. *Maya*, dear, it is all *maya.*'"

I turned my head, eyebrows slightly raised, to get a good look at the animated face of this unusual singer, my companion of the hour, Rowena Plink.

She went on. "You see, my mother has a PhD in Comparative Religion. *Maya* is a concept in Hinduism, the power of illusion. We can believe so strongly at times in things that turn out to be complete illusions, and sometimes even terrible corruptions. Jane loves using that word. *Maya* this, *maya* that—she's constantly cautioning me and my brother, even now, years later! The Buddhists use the term too: it pretty much means deceit, pretending to have qualities you in fact lack."

"Fascinating! I've heard about *karma*, but *maya*, that's new…"

"The Asian religions are *tuned-in,* they really are."

I nodded, and we walked on slowly towards the park. A small ambulance screamed down Broadway behind us, and we each briefly covered our ears.

"But I really should have majored in French," Rowena remarked.

"French?"

"And become a French teacher. I'm good at foreign languages, as most singers are. Very good ear, able to reproduce subtle sounds well. And I love France, love literature, love travel, too! Teaching French would have been so much more satisfying than pursuing music professionally. A stable little job, maybe with junior and senior high-school students, or better yet, at a small college. Summers free! Then I could have sung in choirs just avocationally. There are so many opportunities for good part-time singers."

By this time we had reached leafy, green Riverside Park and had turned to stroll in a southerly direction, the grey-brown Hudson sparkling on our righthand side.

"Listen, sorry," said Rowena. "I don't want to take up too much of your time because I know you must be devastated about Frances—"

"She's much, much better, in fact," I said and then bit my lip, wondering whether I should have kept that piece of information to myself.

"Oh! Wonderful! So she is awake now? I heard she was completely out, just tragically, awfully out, lying there in a white bed in a white room. Caspar visited once, I believe, and he mentioned it to me."

"She is…coming around. She is very weak, she wakes up for a few seconds, then dozes off again and we all panic, then she tends to come around again very briefly much later in the day," I lied, feeling terribly uncomfortable but needing to keep Frances's progress to myself. "But the doctor is very hopeful, says she's on the road back, and she'll make it."

"What a relief!" cried Rowena sincerely, and I was heartened. I could not help but warm to her.

I asked her, "So do you know Caspar well? He runs the Saint Bede's community chorus, right?"

"Right, he does, along with Doug. No, I can't say I know him well."

I waited for her to go on. As the pause continued, I said tentatively, "As you mentioned, Caspar did come to visit Frances in the hospital once, and he and I chatted for a while. Quite a dashing young gentleman, and he seemed quite nice."

Rowena sighed. "Good looks and charm can get you a certain distance. They give you a leg up in the world of the arts, for sure. But I'll tell you, Phoebe, for a conductor, great keyboard skills really have to be part of the package, and steely concentration. Sometimes Averill puts Caspar solely in charge of rehearsing one of the choir's pieces—you probably know that sometimes choir and chorus team up to sing, with the kids, too, but many pieces are selected for choir only, the harder pieces. Let's just say that Caspar needs a lot of work in the keyboard-sight-reading realm, accompanying skills, you know, and sometimes his focus wavers during a piece and he loses the beat."

I just nodded but silently recalled that Caspar himself, during our long conversation in the hospital cafeteria, had confessed to this very weakness in his abilities.

Rowena went on. "Of course, Caspar is still a student. In whatever case, Averill seems to adore him, has him running right and left assisting him not only at the church but at his other gigs."

"Averill is Caspar's teacher, too, I know." I thought of the conversations I'd had with both Victor and Everild, as well as Frances's many emails, and silently wondered what Rowena might have to add to what I already knew in this domain.

"Yes, so of course it would be hard for Caspar to decline to carry out these other tasks. I just hope that nothing… Well, who knows. It's a free world. My pal Erin actually went to coffee with Caspar once—I think she was a little smitten with him—but nothing came of that. She confessed to me a couple weeks later that she would have liked to get to know Caspar better, that he'd been rather flirtatious with her, but after that one coffee he seemed to cool on her. She felt a little hurt, actually. She told me she wasn't in fact sure that Caspar wasn't gay himself, like Averill."

I bit my lip, did not offer what I knew, and let Rowena go on.

"Erin told me that although Saint Bede's is Episcopalian, as you know, Caspar had told her he was Roman Catholic, from a Catholic family. She's actually started to think that he may be a bit of a trickster, presenting a dashing sort of image, flirting with women, and with men, too, but maybe actually being a sort of monastic type."

"No! Really?"

"Yes. It's possible. You know the Roman Church—one of my aunts turned Catholic—the mystique of celibacy, self-sacrifice, piety, devotion…"

"Or maybe he just hasn't found the right woman?"

Rowena paused to consider, then suggested, "Or both?"

I smiled. "True. People are so complex. I don't have much experience with Roman Catholicism. Our family has always been Episcopalian, but actually mostly lapsed, I'm afraid. Frances is the only one who has made her way back to the church at this point."

Rowena nodded. "Anyway, what I *really* wanted to tell you about today is something else. I don't know exactly where the police investigation is right now—"

"Rather stalled out, I think."

"Okay. This is what I heard today, and I just had to tell someone about it. When I saw you leaving church today, I thought I'd start with you."

"I'm all ears, Rowena. Fire away."

"Well, after our rehearsal today I heard a conversation between Vincent and Victor. It was a bit hot in the hall, and some of us after robing up went up and out to the courtyard for a bit of air. We had about twelve minutes before we had to reassemble to process in for the service. I first went to the ladies and then walked out and headed for a shady tree: you may know the grounds a bit, that huge old oak with the iron bench beneath it."

"Yes, I know where you mean."

"I got there and noticed Vincent and Victor on the other side, practically hidden by the huge trunk. They didn't see me arrive, pretty sure, because they were wrapped up in heated conversation and I overheard quite a nasty, short argument." My eyes widened and I remained perfectly silent. "They were discussing Claire—pretty sure of it. They were talking in a hushed tone, but I heard Victor say, 'A woman has free choice after, all. She wasn't your property!' Then Vincent said, 'You knew I was dating her. Then that little *party* you held. You plied her with drinks. You invited her to sing with you at the piano. When I arrived—you told me your gathering started an hour later than it actually did, didn't you?—there you were, cozying up to her.' Victor snapped, 'Look, everyone knows you are a temperamental son of a bitch. If she liked me more than you, it just shows she had really good taste.' Then Vincent said something really terribly rude, which I won't repeat. Well, as much as I wanted to hear everything being said behind that tree, at that point it was getting late, and I quietly got up to go back to the church. Once I was a certain distance away from the tree, I glanced and saw that the two guys had also started to head back, and Vincent actually *punched* Victor on the arm, hard!"

"Wow—definitely no love lost between those two!"

"Right. None at all. So here's my thought. I may be crazy, but what all this made me think was that Vincent was clearly insanely angry at Victor for luring Claire away from him, and he knew, or was pretty sure, that Victor was going to swing by to get Claire after her Thursday rehearsal."

"*That* Thursday? That terrible Thursday night when—"

"*That* Thursday, yes."

I gulped and waited for her to go on. What plagued my mind was the fact that Claire and Frances, with their slim figures and long dark hair, resembled each other to such a degree that from the back in a poorly lighted location, they could easily have been mistaken one for the other.

"I think *both* those guys showed up that Thursday night to see Claire, and then had a big old fight."

"Right in the hall?" I asked incredulously. "But all the other chorus singers would have been there, too, leaving rehearsal!"

"Yes, but the two guys may have drawn Claire aside, asked for a brief chat, and waited until the hall was empty."

"At which point…"

"I don't know, but after hearing this really unnerving conversation between those two, and seeing Vincent punch Victor, I just have a very bad feeling. I needed to tell someone."

"I'm glad you told *me,* Rowena. I think we should go to Detective Morales, and you can tell him everything. I know everyone at Saint Bede's has been questioned, but…"

"We choir members were questioned only very briefly. We talked about that in the days following among ourselves: since we don't rehearse Thursday nights, and since apparently no one reported seeing any of us around, we were all dismissed from being any kind of suspects in these cases. But I really have a terrible feeling…"

Another siren wailed as a flashing police car sped by along Riverside Drive. We rose from the park bench to take our separate ways.

"I will call you tomorrow morning, Rowena—may I?"

Rowena looked at the ground for a moment and then said, "Of course."

13 ✠ May 17

At about 9:00 a.m. today I called Rowena—no answer. Deciding to try her again in an hour, I headed out to the hospital, my mind swirling with Sunday's conversations. I wondered how exactly I was going to manage to hone in any further on what transpired the night of April 22. I dearly hoped that Rowena would not fail to come with me to meet again with Detective Morales.

When I entered Frances's room, there was the man himself at my sister's bedside, appearing just on the point of leaving.

"Phoebe!" said Frances with large eyes, looking up at me, a half-eaten cup of vanilla pudding in front of her. "This is Detective Pandolfo Morales." To him she said, "My older sister, Mrs. Phoebe Overbridge."

"Sir," I said simply, not sure whether to acknowledge that we had met before.

"Mrs. Overbridge," said the detective, stretching out a hand to shake.

"I've been of no help, Phoebe," said Frances. "I told Detective Morales what I told you the other day. I just can't remember anything about the end of that rehearsal, what happened to me. It's a blank."

"It's okay, my dear. Somehow we will get to the bottom of this, I am sure."

I paused a moment and then said, "Frances, and Detective Morales, I need to tell you that these past weeks, when Frances was unconscious, I have actually managed to talk in some depth with many of the people at Saint Bede's."

Frances's eyebrows shot up, and Pandolfo Morales frowned slightly and blinked his eyes. I quickly went on. "Being here in New York, waiting for Frances to recover, I figured I had to do *something,* so I've attended the Sunday services, and I've had a number of private conversations. I really think at this point that I need to tell you a few bits and pieces I've picked up that you may not know, Detective Morales."

"My sister the sleuth!" cried Frances. "Phoebe, you never cease to amaze!"

Detective Morales responded evenly, "Well, of course. I have to leave just now—precinct just paged me—but Mrs. Overbridge, would you be able to come to the station tomorrow morning around 9:30?"

So that was arranged.

After Detective Morales left, I went down to the cafeteria for a cup of tea and to try Rowena again: she answered, and she agreed to come with me tomorrow.

For the rest of the day I sat with Frances, who was happily on to semi-solid foods, feeling as tired as I'd ever been in my life, but summoning the energy to tell her what I'd been up to during the long weeks of her slumber.

14 ✠ May 21

While Frances has been steadily, magnificently regaining perfect health, I have for the past four days been down doing battle with some horrendous microbe. Rowena Plink and I did go speak with Detective Morales on the 18th. She repeated to him what she'd witnessed on Sunday near the oak tree between Vincent and Victor, and then she left, with our thanks. I spent another forty-five minutes with the detective, who dutifully listened and jotted down notes as I recounted to him my bits and pieces. Then, via the drugstore, I staggered slowly back to the subway with bags containing a box of tissues, a bottle of acetaminophen, a jar of Tiger Balm muscle rub, a packet of Imodium tabs, and two liters of green sports drink. Once home and medicated, I climbed into bed and passed out. The stress of the last few weeks apparently at last took its toll on every part of me—but only after Frances had awakened. Maybe that's how these things work.

I am almost fine again, just five pounds lighter, I would say, which seems to suit me. I feel a bit weak, but I think regular walks should solve that.

I stayed away from the hospital, of course, until this afternoon, where, entering Frances's room at about 3:30, I found a radiant-looking Dr. Benedetto Lasso at the bedside of a euphorically grinning Frances Whitestone. Just moments before, he had personally accompanied her two circuits around that floor of Saint Raphael's in order to be assured of her muscle strength and sense of balance. Yes, Frances was up and *walking!* Dr. Lasso could not be happier with how seemingly perfectly Frances has risen from her comatose state, and a few scans and tests have confirmed that she has suffered no lasting damage. I am tempted to shout out *Hallelujah!* Our mother would be pleased with this exclamation, I think, rest her soul.

Now that I am over that nasty bug, Frances will be coming home tomorrow! This evening, therefore, will be devoted to deep cleaning and laundry, as I have let Frances's apartment descend into a horrifically disheveled state. By bedtime, it will be pristine and welcoming once more, ready for her miraculous homecoming.

15 ✠ May 22

Both of us were lighter and a bit slower, my sister and I, as we took our first walk together in New York. But what a splendid day all round! The discharge from Saint Raphael's went smoothly, and on the way home, just before the subway station, we stopped at a stand to buy fresh apricots and strawberries. After sourdough toast and herb omelets that I magically whipped up, Frances and I took a leisurely walk along the tree-lined paths in Riverside Park under a warm and healing sun, and then sat on a bench eating the fresh fruit and watching the world go by. The fact that we were still in the dark about what exactly happened the night of April 22 did not dampen our joy in simply being alive and healthy!

But of course, later on during the evening our conversation returned to Saint Bede's and the puzzle still facing us. To my surprise, Frances wants to go to church tomorrow! It is the annual celebration of their patron saint, she tells me, the Venerable Bede, revered Benedictine scholar monk who hailed from the Kingdom of Northumbria long, long, long ago. His day is actually May 25, but they celebrate this so-called

Doctor of the Church on the Sunday closest to that date.

Naturally, if Frances wants to attend, I'm completely on board. But pondering this, I wonder how the various staff and the choir will react to seeing Frances in the congregation. With relief and delight, I hope. Frances is glad that chorus is finished for the year, says that her lungs feel out of shape for singing. She admits, too, that although she misses the church, she also, quite naturally, feels a twinge of apprehension.

16 ✠ May 23

Father August Bakewell was the first to spot Frances and me as we entered Saint Bede's Church this morning. We arrived twenty minutes early just as the rector was climbing up into the pulpit, where, with a man in a brown uniform, he began tapping perplexedly at the microphone. Once it was apparently working properly, Father Bakewell glanced out, saw us, and hurried down and over to our pew.

"Can this be?" he cried. "Frances, how *wonderful* to have you back!" A genuine smile beamed across his thin face as he stretched out a hand to my sister and nodded to me.

"Thank God, Father Bakewell," responded Frances. "Thank God."

"Indeed. Father Sauer!" he called as that priest was entering just then at the side door. "Radcliffe, look who's here!"

Father Radcliffe Sauer's eyes widened behind his thick, black-framed glasses and his lips parted as he paused briefly before walking briskly over to join us. He, too, then stretched out a friendly hand as he cried, "Welcome back, dear Frances! All the saints rejoice!" We all smiled. He then added, "You are a brave lady, I also must say," at which remark Father Bakewell let out a little bark of surprise.

"Nonsense, Father Sauer," he commented. "There is nothing to be afraid of in attending an eleven-o'clock Eucharist."

"I did not say 'afraid.' I said 'brave.' You must concede that it is brave to return to a place the last memory of which is not so very pleasant."

"Actually," said Frances, "I have no memory of anything that happened that night, other than the rehearsal itself. I have been trying and trying to summon back any recollections about what happened as I left the rehearsal, but it's a complete blank."

Both priests remained silent for a second or two, their faces frozen in smiles that could be called cordial. Then Father Bakewell plunged on. "You know how devastated we've been over all that. I *hope* you know that. Claire's funeral took place last week, back in Montreal. We—the clergy—sent a huge bouquet of flowers to her family. We have not heard back. I don't suppose we will, unless and until these crimes are solved. We felt we had to do something to express our sorrow and grief."

Frances and I stood silently for several moments with eyes cast down, as did the two priests. Then Father Sauer said, "We are having a community lunch after the service today for the whole parish. The annual Feast of Saint Bede, you know, our patron saint, the Venerable. A potluck sort of affair, but we have some very talented cooks in this congregation, and we've brought in some wine, too. I hope you both will stay and join us for that."

"We'd love to," responded Frances. "It will be…"

"In the hall, just below. It's the only space large enough to accommodate such a large crowd."

I felt a pang of unease, remembering only too sharply that it was in the hall that Claire's body was found.

"The staff have set up tables, chairs, flowers, whatnot—that old hall can be transformed quite well into a festive space, actually," added Father Bakewell.

"Wonderful, see you there," I murmured, as the two priests looked at their watches and moved off quickly to prepare for the eleven-o'clock service.

*

At lunch, standing at one of the long, white-clad, flower-adorned tables, reaching for a stuffed mushroom, I said to Frances, "How does it feel to be in this old hall?"

Lively Baroque chamber music was filling the air at medium volume, piped in via a sound system on a small corner table.

"A bit peculiar, I'll admit," she said, popping a red grape into her mouth.

"I agree that you are rather brave, you know."

"Have to get back on the horse after you've fallen off."

"Very wise."

"Why *hello!*" cried a voice behind us, and we turned to see the striking form of the slim, dark-haired assistant choirmaster, Caspar Lang.

"Caspar!" cried Frances, and they embraced warmly.

"So fantastic to see you, Frances," he said with a wide and winning smile. "I knew you would pull through." He beamed at me, too, and I beamed back.

As Caspar and Frances stood facing each other, I saw a tear suddenly trickle down her face. "Poor Claire. So horrible. Here I am, and dear Claire…"

"It's truly appalling," agreed Caspar. "Unfathomable."

At that moment the music director Averill Page strode up quickly to Caspar's side. "Cappy—oh, Phoebe…and *Frances!* Welcome back! How wonderful! My goodness, here you are."

We both smiled broadly at Averill, and Frances said softly, "I am grateful to be back."

"Indeed, indeed. You look well! Forgive me, sorry, but Caspar, a few urgent issues with evensong later on—would you come to my office in, say, fifteen minutes?"

Caspar nodded, and Averill sped off up the stairs out of the hall.

Turning back to Caspar, I said, "I hope this doesn't become one of those unsolved 'cold cases' you hear about. I guess you have those here in New York."

"Everywhere, really," responded Caspar quickly. "Don't worry, I have faith that the truth will come to light soon. As Julian says, 'All shall be well, and all shall be well, and all manner of thing shall be well.'"

"That's one of my favorites!" cried Frances.

"Julian?" I asked.

"Julian of Norwich," answered Frances. "A medieval nun and mystic."

"An anchorite, very solitary," added Caspar. "She suffered a terrible illness at a young age, which only increased her great faith."

"The days of the Plague, you know, the Black Death," said Frances.

"Goodness!"

"She survived and wrote a very important spiritual work, *Revelations of Divine Love,*" said Caspar.

Frances added, "The first English book we know about written by a *woman,* too!"

"Both Catholics and Anglicans revere her as a saint," said Caspar.

"You two are certainly a wealth of spiritual knowledge," I said, smiling. They beamed back at me.

Grey-haired Father Martyn Blum appeared at our side, and as he did so, Caspar said, "Excuse me, but the boss calls! I'll see you again soon, I hope, Frances!" And he strode off towards the stairs after a friendly wave of the hand.

"He *is* adorable," I murmured to Frances, whose face was bright and happy.

"Frances, dear, welcome back!" said Father Blum. "It is a true joy to see you here."

"Father Blum!" Frances and I chimed simultaneously.

"I'm glad to see that the weight of the past is not impeding you from striding forward in the present."

"Elegantly put, Father Blum," responded Frances. "Which isn't to say that I'm not a bit nervous just the same."

"Courage is not the absence of fear, but rather the assessment that…"

At that moment my fork flipped and a blob of garlic hummus flew out and splatted onto the floor. "Oh dear!" I cried. "What an oaf I am!"

"Let me," said Frances, beginning to stoop.

"No, let *me,*" said a tall black man dressed in an attractive pale-yellow linen suit, coming to the rescue. He bent down with impressive agility for a man of his age, which looked to be mid-fifties, used a pink napkin to scoop up and crumple the spill with lightning speed, and then tossed it in a soaring arc into a bin several yards away as if it were a tiny basketball.

As he turned to Frances and me smiling warmly, we gave him profuse thanks, and he said, *"Avec plaisir.* How do you do? I am Cedric Cadichon. I work in the rectory."

"Cedric," I repeated, my eyes widening and a sudden rush of blood coming to my face. Trying to master my surprise, I spluttered, "Very kind of you, very gentlemanly, we…"

"I was just checking that we have enough drinks out, wine and so forth, Perrier, some ginger ale. You know this is our annual feast day."

"Yes, indeed," I said. "Cedric, it's very good to meet you. I'm Phoebe Overbridge, from California, and this is my sister Frances Whitestone, who sings in the chorus."

Cedric's jaw dropped visibly and he took a step to the side. "Frances, *mon Dieu!* I am pleased to meet you." He swallowed and shifted on his feet and then added, as if in a daze, "You are Frances, then. Of course I heard what happened. And *quel miracle,* you are here once more! You…you have not been in the chorus long, I think?"

Frances smiled and said, "I began last September. I've never been to the rectory, so…"

"C'est ça. And I usually attend the early service here. But of course, I heard…"

"Thank you sincerely for your concern, Cedric. I'm absolutely fine now, thank God. Have you worked long at Saint Bede's?"

"I arrived only a year ago January. I am from Haiti."

"From Haiti!" said Frances with enthusiasm. "Oh, how lovely. I love the Caribbean, and I love hearing French spoken. I've never been to Haiti, but we've been to Guadeloupe, haven't we, Phoebe? With Aunt Leslie, back in, oh, was it 2003? Our aunt absolutely loves the Caribbean and each summer visits a different island for a week."

"Yes, it was 2003," I confirmed. "A beautiful trip. Perfect weather there, really, if you don't mind a bit of humidity…"

"And the occasional hurricane—and earthquake," said Cedric somberly. "It must be added."

"Yes, of course. I'm sorry. Terrible stuff. Forgive me, I wasn't thinking. I know Haiti has suffered some big ones."

"Disasters," said Cedric. "Destruction and death on a horrifying scale. Hurricanes, floods—never-ending. I was an English teacher in a village near Port-au-Prince. Many of my students over the years died in these tragedies. And colleagues. Finally, I'd had enough. I have several cousins here in New York. I came up after the earthquake, the big one, the monster. Thank God my cousins were here. And I got a job quickly here at the church."

"You are lucky," I agreed.

"Very blessed, yes," said Cedric, glancing to his side as Father Blum, who had remained standing near us, smiled and glided off to mingle with other parishioners. "I would of course like to return to teaching, but I am older now and, well, I'm blessed to have *any* job. The clergy are very good people."

Cedric moved two inches closer to me and said softly, "I should…there is something I need to talk with you about. You and Frances." His face had contracted into an expression of considerable tension. "May I…?"

Frances and I looked at him with thinly veiled dread. "Of course," said Frances.

"I am coming back with more white wine in two minutes. Just stay around this table and then we'll…we'll just sit agreeably along the side there, as many people are doing."

Once Cedric had dashed off, I said in a very soft voice to Frances as I reached for another mushroom, "You remember what Delroy told us, two of the clergy and me, about the slick spot on the floor the morning he discovered Claire's body."

"Of course I do."

"Well, we must remember to ask Cedric about that, somehow."

"Is it wise talking with him right here?"

"He probably can't get away easily. We'll just…just look natural, sociable. Hopefully. It's pretty crowded in here."

When Cedric reappeared, having placed three bottles of Chilean Sauvignon Blanc on each of the two long tables, he helped himself to wine and a small plate of delectables, as Frances and I did the same. We three then smiled cordially and walked slowly to a line of grey folding chairs along one wall, many of which were occupied by older, white-haired parishioners chatting and holding cheery blossom-patterned paper plates heaped with food on their laps. As we lowered ourselves into the hard metal chairs, we casually edged a very small distance away from our neighbors, and Frances raised a toast: "Here's to the Venerable Bede!"

"Indeed, to Saint Bede!" said I.

"Mesdames," began Cedric softly. "I have very little time to sit with you, but I must tell you. It has been wrong of me to remain silent."

We looked at him with wide-open eyes.

"Please do not show your emotions, ladies, if possible." We nodded, took small sips of wine, and he went on. "I came to this hall the night before Claire's body was found." I swallowed hard and Frances let out a short cough as we kept our eyes riveted on Cedric. "I was bringing some leftover pasta from the dinner the clergy had enjoyed that evening. It would be wrong to waste it—I do this as often as I can, put foil containers and bags in the fridge here, and they add it to what they serve the poor and homeless guests who come to the Saturday soup kitchen."

"I see," I said, trying to quash my impatience. "I think that is admirable, Cedric. Bravo."

"En fait, there is a poor man who comes directly round to the rectory from time to time, and, as I recall, I gave him a small leftover bag that evening before I set out for the hall."

Cedric glanced as imperceptibly as he could in a wide arc around the room and then continued. "The rector might have no problem with this. Then again, he might. Father Blum found out one day—"

At this utterance, my mind flashed back to Craig Scranch's story of how he had been detained by the police but quickly cleared by both Father Blum and Cedric.

"—but when he saw my great distress, he assured me that he would not tell Father Bakewell. This job means the world to me, coming from Haiti, as I told you. And yet, at the very same time, coming from a place so wracked with poverty and despair, I could not bear to see good food wasted."

I was nearly fainting from anxiety, and Frances looked much the same. I simply said, "Completely understandable. Of course it is."

"But my life means nothing if I don't tell the whole truth now," continued Cedric, his paper plate shaking slightly in his hands.

We waited.

"That night, around 9:10, I went over and into the hall the back way, as I do on these errands, straight down into the basement."

"Not via the church's south side door?" asked Frances.

"No, the back way is more direct and discreet, and the hall door there is not in view of the rectory or the courtyard."

"Yes, understandable, I see."

"It's a bit of a maze down there, many rooms. So as I was walking along a corridor with several foil boxes, I heard voices, people arguing.

I slowed my steps because, well, of course I try to transfer these leftovers when no one is around."

"Could you hear what was said?"

"Yes, quite clearly. As you can tell today, sound bounces off these walls—only the ceiling is somewhat insulated. One person, a man, said softly yet with a distinct edge, 'We *cherish* this service. The parish cherishes it. It has become a tradition here.'"

Frances asked tensely, "Could you tell who was speaking?"

"Not just then. A woman then responded, 'It is *barbaric*. The animals don't want to be here. And circuses are no longer in vogue!' The man barked, 'The Feast of Saint Francis is in no way a circus, young lady!' She then said, 'But it *is*. You truck the large animals in from upstate, you make them stand on the cold stone floor, they stomp, they moan, surrounded by hundreds of dogs and cats barking and howling, with clouds of incense clogging the already close air—not one creature in that nave, large or small, is happy! All to the wild and wooly sounds of that disturbing mass always on the program. I'm sorry, but this is *animal exploitation* on a grand scale, and you perpetuate it year after year simply to bring in the crowds and bring in the *cash!*'"

Frances and I could not help gasping.

"Please, eat calmly from your plates," said Cedric, as at the other side of the hall, Father Bakewell came back into view.

"I will get straight to the point," said Cedric, sweat now beading his brow. "I heard a sharp cry, a scuffle, and then a dreadful *crack,* and at that point, I simply had to move forward to see what on earth was going on. As I quietly rounded a corner, I saw a man running to the end of the hall, to the stairs."

"The south stairs?" I asked.

"Yes. He ran up those stairs two by two, out of sight. He did not see me."

"And that man was…?" I asked in a nearly strangled voice.

"Averill Page, the music director."

"Are you sure?" asked Frances.

"I am sure. I had already recognized his voice. He comes to dine at the rectory often with the clergy. I am very sure it was he. As I approached the piano, quaking, I saw the body of a woman face down, her dark hair splayed out. As I bent down towards her, I dropped a container and pasta spilled out. I panicked. I froze for a moment in the silence. I saw that the woman was completely still."

"Claire," Frances whispered.

"Then I somehow found my feet and rushed to the kitchen area, put the boxes in the fridge, grabbed a towel, and returned. I quickly wiped up the spill, what I could see of it."

"And then?" I asked.

"I knew she was dead. I'd heard the loud crack, and I could see blood pooling around her head, her hair gone very wet. It was a terrible sight that will haunt me for the rest of my life."

"Jesus Christ," I uttered, and Frances briefly put her head in her hands.

"I am sorry. So very sorry. I left her there, I threw the towel in the bin—no, there was no blood on it that I could see—and I quickly returned to the rectory."

"And you told…?"

"No one," he whispered mournfully.

"No one," Frances and I murmured simultaneously, incredulously.

"This is my sin," said Cedric. "I lied to the police. I was terrified for myself, for my job, for my life. I knew there was nothing anyone could do for the woman, and I knew the maintenance guys would find her in the morning. I told no one about this, about what I had heard and seen in the hall. There were no witnesses except myself. Why would anyone believe me, a poor immigrant from Haiti, accusing the esteemed music director of a grand church? I feared that if I spoke up, it would be *I* who would be accused—and convicted. But now my conscience is ripping me to shreds. Especially after meeting you, Frances."

Tears began to pool in all our eyes.

Frances said in a hushed and distraught tone, "Phoebe, you told me that while I was in the coma, I surfaced slightly one day and murmured something about someone 'rushing.' So, then…it must have been *Averill* who rushed by me. Wasn't

I…yes, yes! I was going to wait for Claire up in the fresh air..."

"Of course, I never saw you, Frances, since I returned immediately along the *back* path to the rectory," said Cedric. He glanced briefly around the festive hall once more and said, "Please compose your faces, *Mesdames.* I must go."

"Yes," I said, my brain spinning. "Yes, you must. But—you will now tell the police, Cedric?"

"I have to. I will," he said lifting himself despondently from his chair.

At that moment, as a Telemann horn concerto began gayly in the background, Everild Dunne appeared, marching directly toward our little threesome with a look of complete devastation on her face. "Cedric," she said urgently when she reached us, "please come quickly to help. Averill has had a terrible accident."

17 ✠ May 25

This evening, Tuesday, clear and mild after a heavy downpour, found Frances and me seated in familiar, small upholstered armchairs in the Saint Bede's rectory parlor, assembled in a circle with Fathers Bakewell, Sauer, and Blum, and Everild Dunne.

Father Bakewell had summoned us all there. "My dear friends, we have more clarity now, and Father Blum and I have spoken with the police. We will be meeting later with others of our staff, but…I need to inform you first, right now, about Averill Page's injuries and…well, let me just explain it all as best I can."

Frances and I looked at each other briefly with doubt and worry but then focused fully on the rector.

"Averill took a very hard fall on Sunday, as I think you all know. Rushing to his office, he stumbled badly—apparently on a protruding tree root—and fell headlong on the cement walkway, severely gashed his right ear, broke one wrist trying to cushion his fall, and also injured a knee. We rushed him to Saint Raphael's, where they did various emergency surgeries—took about six hours in all. I won't go into all the medical details, but suffice it to say that once the general anesthetic wore off, they put him immediately on morphine for the post-surgical pain—quite searing, apparently. Can you imagine: a world-renowned organist and conductor suffering a broken wrist, a torn knee ligament, a gashed ear, and…more? Tragic."

Everyone remained silent and gazed down mournfully at the mock-Persian carpet.

Father Bakewell went on. "But it must have been the heavy doses of morphine that did it. That…brought the whole sorry business to light at last."

"Rather like *in vino veritas,*" mused Father Sauer.

"From my hospital visits generally," added Father Blum, "I can confirm that morphine does have that effect on many people—the words just tumble out, begin to flow, whatever might be pressing on the mind and heart." We all nodded appreciatively at the expertise of the priest in charge of counseling and pastoral care.

Everild asked the rector, "What was it he said about *karma?*"

Father Bakewell coughed and said, "Yes. Well, as Martyn and I sat at his bedside yesterday evening, that morphine pump erect at his side, Averill suddenly blurted out, '*Karma* wins! All get their just reward!' We didn't know what to make of this, just looked at him silently, expectantly. He said, 'I was the one.' Tears began to gush from his eyes, and we asked him what on earth he meant. Then he told us the whole story."

All eyes in the parlor remained riveted on the rector.

"I'll summarize as best I can. Martyn, help me out if I falter in some detail. Well, on Thursday, April 22, when Averill got home in the taxi from the opera feeling very ill, it was just about 9:00. He staggered, he said, straight to the hall, looking to speak briefly to Doug about subbing for him at the event the next day…"

"You mean the Feast of Saint George service, I assume," said Father Sauer.

"Exactly. But Doug had already left rehearsal, had apparently dismissed it early, and there were only a few chorus singers still exiting the hall. Averill then went to the men's room, he said, and threw up. Came out and just one woman remained, Claire, the alto, who seemed to want to talk to him. 'Stupid fanatical bitch!' Averill cried to Martyn and me, tears streaming down his cheeks. She apparently poked Averill on the chest after delivering a rant about the annual Saint Francis service and animal abuse, and she began to turn away from him. He said he had felt 'so unbelievably…' What was the word he used, Martyn?"

"Incensed."

"Yes: 'so unbelievably incensed' that he pushed her—'as hard as I could!'"

At that point in Father Bakewell's narration, gasps were heard all around and several female hands shot up to mouths, while Father Sauer pronounced, "Simply appalling, unspeakable. How little we know what lies within a man…"

Father Bakewell continued. "All this is indeed very wrenching to relate. Averill lay there in bed, bandaged and bruised, his face red as a beet as words continued to gush out of him. He then absolutely broke down, wailing, 'That wasn't really me! I didn't mean to, I didn't mean to, I didn't mean to.' Well, as you can imagine, Martyn and I could hardly believe what we were hearing."

Every face in the little parlor had gone very pale, and Father Blum said, "I've been in many extreme situations, but I confess that just then, witnessing the full agony of Averill's state, a man I thought I knew well, I felt my heart was about to drop right out of me!"

Father Bakewell, beads of sweat now breaking out on his thin face, ran a hand across his forehead and then continued. "What was it he said? *Very light?* Oh yes, Averill babbled on that Claire was so much lighter than she looked—she was, as we know, one of those fairly tall but very small-boned people. Averill raged about her pale skin, her long black hair, that she was 'like a fury, a witch, sent to torment' him. It was frankly awful to see the pathetic state he had descended to."

"Sounds like he cracked, as they say," remarked Everild. "He definitely cracked."

"So poor Claire, down she crashed, *hard,* and hit her head on, apparently, a piano leg. Averill couldn't believe it, honestly 'could not believe it.' 'A nightmare, a nightmare,' he kept repeating to us, while also repeating phrases like 'cursed witch,' and 'idiotic woman.'"

We all just moaned and shifted in our chairs.

"Then he turned and ran, he said, and once up and out of the church, there on the path was Frances!"

"Yes, waiting for Claire in the fresh air, I've remembered that now," she confirmed.

"He said that he felt he was losing his mind. What was *Frances* doing there? Claire's friend. He said that it flashed into his mind that she also had failed to participate in the Saint Francis service earlier that year. He felt woozy and about to be sick again. *'You snake,'* he muttered, trying to stagger past her as quickly as he could."

"Snake?" I asked. "He called my sister a *snake*?"

Father Bakewell nodded with shame. "His tongue was fully loosened at that point—he maundered on in a most pathetic manner, told us everything through his tears, his dripping nose... It was extremely difficult to attend to this…this horrific confession, there at Averill's bedside."

Father Blum agreed fully.

The rector continued. "You, Frances, apparently began to raise your arm at that point…"

"Understandably, in self-protection," I interjected.

"...and Averill said he made a motion as if to swat you away. Something apparently caught on his fancy wristwatch just as he passed you, a sleeve or scarf or—"

I interjected, "That black knitted sweater with roses around the sleeves, Frances! You had that on that night—it was in your personal effects bag at the hospital! It's very snagable, yes."

"All right, her sweater sleeve quite probably, then," said Father Bakewell. "And down you went, my poor dear, crashing onto the path! Averill said that he felt he had already gone completely insane. He quickly disentangled his watch, rushed home, vomited once more, and threw himself into bed."

We all waited for what the rector would say next.

"And, obviously, he told no one anything at all."

Father Sauer said, "When August and I got home from the opera just after 10:00, everything was quiet, and we just retired."

Father Blum added, "I was up working, as you also all know, and it was at about 10:20 that I popped over to the church in search of the book I'd left—which is when I came across you, Frances."

I asked Father Bakewell, "But the next day: you did see Averill fairly early in the morning?"

"As I believe I told you, yes, he looked quite a bit the worse for wear, but we chalked that up to his stomach upset of the night before. We were *all* in rather a terrible state at that point, of course. And then very soon after, the ultimate shock came when Delroy came across Claire."

A long pause ensued, and then Father Blum quietly remarked, "And life went on with great confusion and perplexity…"

"Until now," said Frances, and all turned to her and nodded solemnly.

18 ✹ June 1

Within two days, the avid New York media outlets had got hold of the story: the front page of *The New York Post* shouted out, *Renowned maestro descends into real-life inferno: Averill Page confesses to Saint Bede's murder.* On the front page of *The New York Times,* albeit below the fold, ran a story entitled *Injured conductor and organ virtuoso Averill Page confesses to murder from hospital bed.* Tweets and posts flooded social media as journalists around the country enjoyed a lush field day of reporting on how, so very tragically, the world of classical and choral music had seen one of its brightest stars explode into the void.

But Frances and I, well and truly over it all, continued packing as we sang a song we had known all our lives:

California, here I come!
Right back where I started from!
Where bowers of flowers bloom in the spring;
Each morning, at dawning,
Birdies sing and ev-er-y-thing.
A sun-kissed miss says, "Don't be late!"
That's why I can hardly wait!
Open up that Golden Gate:
California, here I come! *

**Song written by Buddy DeSylva, Joseph Meyer, & Al Jolson, 1921.*

Made in the USA
Monee, IL
11 December 2023

48967323R00125